KU-496-491

TRACK DOWN THE DEVIL

TRACK DOWN THE DEVIL

by

Greg Mitchell

Dales Large Print Books
Long Preston, North Yorkshire,
BD23 4ND, England.

British Library Cataloguing in Publication Data.

Mitchell, Greg
  Track down the devil.

  A catalogue record of this book is
  available from the British Library

  ISBN   978-1-84262-708-2 pbk

BOLTON LIBRARIES

137 7302 X

MAGNA 2.109109

F £11.99

First published in Great Britain in 2008 by Robert Hale Limited

Copyright © Greg Mitchell 2008

Cover illustration © Gordon Crabb by arrangement with
Alison Eldred

The right of Greg Mitchell to be identified as the author of this
work has been asserted by him in accordance with the
Copyright, Designs and Patents Act, 1988

Published in Large Print 2009 by arrangement with
Robert Hale Limited

All Rights reserved. No part of this publication may be
reproduced, stored in a retrieval system, or transmitted in any
form or by any means, electronic, mechanical, photocopying,
recording or otherwise without the prior permission of the
Copyright owner.

Dales Large Print is an imprint of Library Magna Books Ltd.

Printed and bound in Great Britain by
T.J. (International) Ltd., Cornwall, PL28 8RW

ONE

Josh Baxter rode as comfortably as the hard-seated Morgan saddle on the near-wheel mule would allow but his mind was far from easy. He had been driving a jerkline outfit for Carl Gustavson's freight company for a couple of years, but that day the familiar road seemed somehow to be different. The six-mule team was stepping out smartly, the morning was cool and the real heat of the sun was yet to strike. At another time he might have burst into song or even whistled a tune. But that morning would not be like the others and the mule-skinner drew little comfort from the familiar surroundings.

On either side of the road sagebrush flats stretched away for half a mile to the red walls of the canyon. Where the country began to rise at the base of the rock walls, greasewood and clumps of cactus dotted the sloping ground. The terrain close to the wagon trail looked open but Baxter knew that it was deceptive. The flats were scored deeply by erosion and an army could be hidden in the deep gullies.

Young, red-bearded and powerfully built, the mule-skinner looked as tough as he was and the long-barrelled Colt .44 on his right hip advertised that he was not a man to be taken lightly.

'Be careful,' folks in Santa Rosa had warned him. 'The trail to the railroad is getting too dangerous. Don't go on it alone.' But Baxter had his own ideas and reckoned that the advice did not apply to him. His boss, in the interests of delivering goods on schedule, had left the decision to go or wait to the mule-skinner himself but had let it be known that he preferred not to delay deliveries.

The first sign that he was not alone came when he sighted a puff of dust rising above the flat on his left. The sandy red soil was loose and drifted easily but there was no wind gust to disturb it. Something was moving. It might have been a deer or even a mustang, but given the shortage of good grazing in the area, that was unlikely. Baxter was almost certain that it would have been a shod horse raising the dust. Anxiously he straightened in the saddle and looked about. Though he saw nothing, he knew that the landscape was not as empty as it appeared to be. But he was committed and it was too late to turn around.

As though by magic riders seemed to come out of the ground, five hard-bitten men, unshaven, dusty and heavily armed. With drawn guns they approached and fanned out across the trail in the manner of predatory animals about to attack.

Tim Cleary reined in his dapple-grey horse and dismounted at the hitching rack outside the low-roofed, adobe building that was the sheriff's office in Santa Rosa, New Mexico. He flipped the reins over the rail, hitched his gunbelt with its holstered Colt into a more comfortable position and strode through the open door of the building. He had enjoyed the ride but now it was time to go to work.

A dark-haired man, a bit older than Cleary's twenty-four years looked up from a desk in the corner of the room. Like many New Mexican lawmen, Lou Braga was part Mexican but he had the blue eyes of his American mother. He had been expecting Cleary so had a fair idea as to his visitor's identity. He wore range clothing but looked a bit too clean and neat for a working cow-hand.

'Sheriff Braga?'

'That's right. What can I do for you?'

'I'm US Marshal Tim Cleary. I wrote to you about the Baxter case.'

Braga rose and extended a hand. 'Pleased to meet you. I'm Lou to anyone on the right side of the law. Help yourself to that spare chair and tell me how I can help with this mess.'

Cleary took a seat, dropped his hat on the floor beside him and said, 'Like my letter mentioned, I'm here to try to find out what happened to the sixty Spencer rifles and the quantity of ammunition that were on Baxter's wagon when he was robbed and probably murdered. They were supposed to be sent back to the Springfield Arsenal after the cavalry detachment over on Salt Plain was issued with the new trapdoor Springfields. The army is doing away with the Spencers but a few people in Washington are rather keen to get them back. The War Department doesn't like government property going missing and the government can't afford to be seen as supplying arms to Mexican revolutionaries.'

'You're a bit late, Tim. I'm pretty sure those rifles will be in Mexico by now,' Braga told him. 'There are plenty of revolutionaries and bandits who would happily buy them. The mules and harness were taken too, but the rest of the freight was only salted hides so the bandits left them. We found a couple of busted boards from the gun cases where the bandits must have broken some open to see what was in them but that was the only trace found.'

'What happened to Baxter?'

Braga frowned. 'We don't know for sure. There were a couple of bullet holes in the wagon and some blood on the ground. He's probably lying dead out in the desert somewhere. I don't know why they didn't leave the body near the wagon, but they didn't.'

'What about tracks?'

'Looked like half-a-dozen or so riders. There were tracks of men and mules all over the area as though they had been galloping about. Maybe it was to confuse anyone trying to follow their trail. In places they had been wiped out by a crazy old Mexican feeding a herd of goats around the area. We managed to pick up a few horse tracks and followed them to the Socorro road but there's a lot of traffic from the mines over that road and the tracks were blotted out. I'm sure though that the gang that stole those rifles is still in the area. There have been stage robberies, horses run off from

11

ranches and food and supplies taken from ranch houses. A couple of lone travellers have been murdered on the trail, too. It's been going on for more than a year now. Probably the one gang is doing it all even though the crimes might be many miles apart. They are not afraid to split up. There can be as few as two men or six or eight depending upon the size of the job. I have been run off my feet and have had posses out so many times that I have trouble getting volunteers now.'

'Do you think the goats were deliberately driven over the tracks to cover them?'

'No. Their owner is crazy and nobody knows what he's likely to do next. I'm sure his part in this is quite innocent. He's a harmless old soul and has lived around here for years.'

'And you have no idea who's behind all this trouble?'

Braga shook his head. 'Not really. Some victims spoke of a well-dressed, well-spoken character who was giving orders, but the description doesn't fit anyone we know. Few words were spoken and all were masked so we are none the wiser about who the leader is.'

'I wonder whether they knew Baxter's

wagon was carrying those rifles,' the marshal said. 'Bandits usually are looking for cash or stuff that's easy to sell. They would not expect to find money on a freight wagon.'

'Maybe they were only after the mules and harness. Good mules are worth a fair bit and harness is not cheap. They might have found the rifles by accident or they might have known about them and already had a market. I've tried to figure every angle but it still has me beat.'

After further short discussion, Cleary rose. 'I'd better get moving. I have to get a hotel room and find a place for my horse. Then I might visit the freight company that Baxter worked for. I expect to be here for a few days, but will add to your problems as little as possible. If you need help, let me know.'

Braga also stood up and took his hat from a rack on the nearby wall. 'I'll help you get settled in and show you where to find Gustavson's freight office. Gustavson himself is away, but Julia Cross runs the office so you're in luck. She's a real honey, smart and good-looking with it.

Santa Rosa was not a big town and few people were about. Consequently it did not take long to arrange lodgings for the marshal and his horse. Braga pointed out the freight company office and then left Cleary to his own devices. The latter was about to enter the building when a horseman passed. He was a type that the marshal instantly recognized. The newcomer was dressed like a cowhand but did not act like one. He was in his late thirties, of medium height and build with a tanned face, lined by the weather. His sandy hair and moustache were neatly trimmed indicating that he had not been living out on the cattle ranges. He wore two guns, had a rifle on his saddle and bestrode a well-conditioned dark brown horse of good breeding. He had the look of a gunman about him and rode alertly, taking in all that he saw around him. There's trouble, Cleary thought, as he walked into the freight office. But he was not responsible for keeping order in the town. Any trouble would be Braga's.

A very attractive, dark-haired young woman walked across to the counter. 'Can I help you?' she asked with a smile that Cleary thought was the best thing he had seen in Santa Rosa. He introduced himself and explained why he was there.

'I'm Julia Cross,' the girl said. 'Mister Gustavson is out of town at present but he

has told me to cooperate with any law officers making enquiries. I have all the company records and will help you all I can.
Where would you like to start?'

The marshal asked the usual questions
about how the transport of the rifles had
been arranged, who had arranged it and
who knew the contents of the boxes. He
learned that the contents had not been
described on the waybills but by the shape
of the boxes and their origin, it was obvious
what they contained.

Cleary scribbled a few notes in his notebook but learned little that he did not
already know. He was loath to end the interview though because he was enjoying Julia's
company. She had a gentle, friendly manner
which was a pleasant contrast to the rough-
hewn characters with whom the lawman
usually had to deal. When the girl suggested
that she make them coffee, he accepted with
alacrity but then suddenly, he was forced to
postpone what he had expected to be a very
enjoyable interlude.

He happened to glance up just in time to
see two more horsemen ride past the door.
They had the same predatory look as the
rider he had seen earlier. One such person
could be trouble but three in the same town

15

at once indicated a looming disaster.

'I'm sorry, Miss Cross, but I have to go,' he said hastily as he rose from his chair and grabbed his hat.

Julie's big blue eyes opened wide in surprise at the lawman's sudden departure.

Looking along the street, he saw no sign of the riders but a man was holding four horses outside the town's only bank. He had not seen the fourth man arrive and hoped that he had not missed others.

The sheriff's office was between him and the bank and Cleary wondered if Braga was aware of the situation. But he need not have worried.

As he drew level with the office, the grim-faced lawman met him at the door. 'Get in here quick.'

'So you saw them?'

'I saw them, but can't do anything while they're still in the bank because other people are in there too. I intend to get them as they are mounting their horses. If you are here to help, grab that other Winchester off my desk. It's fully loaded.'

Cleary ran to the desk, picked up the rifle and hurried back to the door. Because of the angle only one man could shoot from the office entrance. Seeing a solidly built

16

wooden horse trough a couple of yards away at the edge of the street, the marshal decided that he would take up his position there when the action started.

'Try to get the ones with the money,' Braga whispered. 'We have a better chance of getting the others then as they try to pick it up.'

'Are you going to challenge them first?'

'Why waste breath? None of them will surrender peaceably and they outnumber us anyway.'

'Can we count on any support from the town?'

The sheriff looked doubtful. 'Maybe – if Black Baxter's about he'll lend a hand but it could take him a while to get from the freight warehouse. Others might join in if they have guns handy but we can't count on it.' Then he tensed and cocked the rifle in his hands. 'Get ready, the bank door's opening.'

The man holding the horses saw the movement too and led the animals out into the road.

TWO

Suddenly they were on the street, three men with bandannas over the lower halves of their faces, each clutching a revolver. The foremost glared about seeking anyone who might try to bar their progress. The second man carried a pair of bulging saddle-bags over his left arm and headed straight for the horses. The third one backed away, his gun trained on the bank door. The horse-holder, who had now pulled up his own mask, moved forward eagerly to pass the reins to his companions.

'Let's go,' Braga said, as he cocked his rifle and stepped outside.

The bandits saw the movement as the two lawmen emerged from the office. One shouted in alarm and all turned their guns toward the threat.

Braga and Cleary fired almost simultaneously and the man with the saddle-bags was punched backwards into the street. One of his companions, a short, stocky man in a striped shirt fired back and the bullet buried

18

itself in the door jamb beside the sheriff. Then he stooped, grabbed the saddle-bags from the fallen man and disappeared among the plunging horses. For the next few seconds both sides swapped lead taking snap shots at fast-moving targets. The bandits were at a disadvantage as the range was a bit long for their revolvers but the bullets they sent back were accurate enough to gain the lawmen's respect. So far all had missed but not by much.

One of Braga's shots knocked the already mounted man from his horse and the riderless animal collided with the horses that the surviving pair were trying to mount. Knocked to the ground, the fallen bandit stayed there and fired at Cleary as he took refuge behind the trough. The bullet splashed water in the marshal's face but, slowed by the water, it failed to penetrate the solid wooden end of the trough.

Suddenly the loose horses had bolted away. Two dead men were sprawled in the street and another wounded bandit, his six shooter emptied, was raising his hands in submission. 'I give up,' the man called weakly. 'Don't shoot – I'm hit bad.'

'Be careful,' Cleary called to Braga. 'There's another one there somewhere. I reckon he has the money too.'

'He must have ducked down that alley. He won't get far without a horse,' the sheriff replied.

'If you want to secure that prisoner, I'll go after him,' the marshal volunteered.

'Do that, but be careful. I'll get a search organized for that one soon if you can't find him. If you do find him and he won't surrender, just try to pin him down. The town folks will be here soon.'

Cleary waited until Braga called the staggering prisoner away and then went down the alley. It offered no protection for anyone wanting to ambush him so he could hurry along with little risk to himself. The alley led out to open ground behind the buildings. Though relatively flat for a fair distance, it was dotted with mesquite, cactus and tall weeds and offered many places for a fugitive to conceal himself. He was looking about for tracks when a dark-haired man with a rifle emerged from the back of Gustavson's freight depot. The newcomer sighted the lawman and walked rapidly to join him.

'Hi,' he greeted. 'I'm Black Baxter. My real name's Aaron but folks call me Black to distinguish me from my brother who is Red Baxter – or was Red Baxter. I heard the shooting and reckoned Lou could do with a hand. But he has plenty of help now. I would have been here sooner but I had to lock up the freight warehouse before I left.'

Cleary introduced himself and described the missing hold-up man.

'A little *hombre* in a striped shirt with grey pants, a brown hat and big saddle-bags should be fairly easy to spot among the townsfolk,' Baxter said.

The marshal pointed to the landscape away from the town. 'That's where I'd be heading if I was in his boots. It's hard to hide in a town this small. If he can hide out there somewhere there's a chance that he might try to creep back in tonight and steal a horse.'

Baxter nodded his head in agreement.

The pair searched around for a while but found no trace of the missing bandit. A few more gun-toting townsmen joined them but it seemed as though their quarry had sprouted wings. Finally Cleary told the other searchers, 'We haven't found a single track indicating that our man left town. I think he's outsmarted us somehow and got back in.'

Baxter told him, 'If you want to compare notes with Braga, I'll look after things here.

I am a part-time deputy.'

Cleary hurried back because he knew that Braga would be a busy man trying to identify the robbers and at the same time gather witnesses' names. The town's doctor was attending to the captive who was bleeding profusely from a chest wound.

'How is he?' Cleary asked the sheriff.

'He's hit pretty bad and can't or won't talk. What about the one with the money?'

'We can't find hide nor hair of him but he won't get far without a horse. Baxter's organizing a hunt for him. Says he's a part-time deputy. Is he reliable?'

'Very,' Braga confirmed. 'His regular job is minding the Gustavson freight warehouse. It was almost a family affair. Red Baxter, his brother, was Gustavson's best teamster. Aaron has sworn to bring Red's killers to justice. The town council gave me permission to swear him in as a deputy on an as-needs basis. Right now he's needed badly.'

'How can I best help?'

'If you take over the search and send Baxter to me, we can start tying up the loose ends here. When Doc Hadlow finishes patching up our prisoner I'll try to rig up a cell for him where the doc can keep a safe eye on him.'

When Cleary returned to Baxter, he found that the latter had stationed townspeople at strategic points on the town's perimeter and with a couple more well-armed citizens was searching every building and shed as they worked their way through the town. Baxter moaned when Cleary told him that Braga needed him. 'I was hoping he wouldn't call for me. I want to catch up with that thieving coyote because I'm sure he could tell me what happened to Josh. If you corner him, try to take him alive. There are a lot of questions need answering.'

Two hours later, the searchers reached the last building at the end of town, Gustavson's freight warehouse.

Julia looked amused when Cleary returned and explained the purpose of his visit. 'I know now why you so ungraciously turned down my coffee earlier,' she teased. 'It's not often that men run out on me like that.'

'Well, I'm back now, but unfortunately Lou Braga has me working. Have you seen any strangers about?'

The girl shook her head. 'You are the only stranger I've seen today. The business has dropped off a lot since Josh Baxter was killed. Aaron was down at the warehouse. I heard him locking the main doors after the shooting stopped and then saw him run past here with a rifle.'

'Could anyone get into the warehouse?'

'No. Aaron keeps the doors locked whenever he is not there and he carries the keys with him. He's very conscientious and he knows that occasionally we have valuable goods stored there.'

'I don't doubt you, Miss Cross, but I'll have a look at the warehouse just in case our bank robber has broken in and is hiding there. It might be safer too if you close the business for the day and go home. There's a very dangerous man loose around here somewhere.'

'Good luck, Marshal,' Julia said as he left the office.

The freight warehouse had large double doors secured by a sturdy padlock and heavy chain. No forced entry was evident. A smaller rear entrance was locked in a similar manner. The windows were higher than a man on the outside could reach and upon inspection all were found to be intact.

Cleary turned to the pair of volunteers who were assisting him. 'It looks like he got out of town. Let's get horses and see what we can find.'

'But how do we know where to start looking?' one man asked.

'We do a big loop around the entire town and look for any recent tracks coming out of it. He didn't leave by the road. We know that much. Braga saw him ducking down the alley on the western side but with the crooked main street here, he could have gone to where it bends, doubled back and left on the eastern side.'

It took three hours to do two complete circuits of the town. The first one was roughly a quarter of a mile from the buildings but they found no tracks. If the fugitive had escaped he had not travelled that far. The second one was approximately a hundred yards from the structures. Again they found no fresh tracks.

Cleary pushed back his hat and wiped a sweaty forehead with his shirt sleeve. 'I don't know how we missed him,' he told the others. 'I reckon our man is still in town. Let's go back and break the news to Braga.'

They were about to return when Cleary sighted a horseman approaching. He was a small man in a derby hat and wore a long linen duster to protect his dark suit from the red dust. His horse was a fast-walking pinto.

'That's Phil Edison,' one of the volunteers said. 'He's a professional gambler who does the rounds of the towns here. He pretends to be nice and polite but the story is that he's mighty fast with a gun. Folks are a bit careful around him.'

Cleary did not like professional gamblers. Most of those he knew were greedy people who would cheat if the opportunity arose. But he was prepared to take people as he found them. Maybe Edison was different.

'It's not often I get a welcoming committee,' the gambler said as he came abreast of the others. The refined tones were those of an educated man. With a slight smile he added, 'I presume that you gentlemen are not waiting here in the hope of a game of poker. How can I help you?'

Cleary introduced himself and explained what they were doing. He saw no need for secrecy as all of Santa Rosa knew what had occurred.

The gambler could add nothing to what they already knew. He was adamant that he had seen no other travellers on the trail. However, he seemed a little concerned that the bank robbery might have affected the availability of gamblers in town. 'My stay in this place might not be as long as I had originally planned,' he told Cleary as they rode together into Santa Rosa.

The marshal had a hasty meal at the hotel before returning to the sheriff's office, where Braga was assembling the witness statements he had laboriously written during the afternoon. 'Is the prisoner well enough to tell you anything?' he asked.

'Not really,' the sheriff replied. 'The doctor has patched him up and given him something to make him rest. He's going to call back later and check on him. How did you get on?'

'We couldn't find a sign of our missing man. I think he could be in town still, but if he is, he's well hidden. It might be a good idea to keep an eye on any horses that are in town tonight just in case he tries to steal one. By the way – do you know that you have a visitor?'

'I saw Phil Edison riding in. I doubt that he'll find too many customers tonight.'

'It struck me as a bit odd that a well-known gambler can ride safely around country that's infested with bandits. Hold-up men like to pray on gamblers on the usually false assumption that they are carrying a lot of money.'

Braga gave a rueful smile. 'I reckon our local bad boys have their sights set higher than one tinhorn gambler. Clem Summers,

27

over at the bank, reckons they got away with close to five thousand dollars today. He's still checking books and will give me a complete figure in the morning. Luckily no one in the bank was hurt. I have a couple of volunteer deputies coming to relieve me soon and then I'm heading home to get some sleep. I'm so tired I could sleep in the middle of a clump of cactus and not feel it. It's going to be a big day tomorrow.'

But the day was soon to become bigger than either of the lawmen expected.

THREE

Cleary was pulling off his boots when he heard the horse passing in the street below. With idle curiosity he looked out the window of his hotel room. A pinto horse with a rider in a long duster and derby hat was just passing through a pool of light thrown by the lamps shining through the windows of a saloon. Looks like Edison couldn't find any suckers, he told himself. He thought it strange that the gambler should be leaving at such a late hour, but guessed that he might have been staying at one of the ranches just out of town.

Some time later he was awakened by voices in the street. At first he thought it might have been a couple of drunks arguing, but then he heard Braga's voice. Though the words were indistinct, the tone was far from happy. His lawman's instincts told Cleary that there was trouble so he rolled out of bed and dressed quickly. He was still buckling on his gunbelt when he emerged from the hotel.

'I was just about to wake you up,' Braga

29

told him. 'Our bank robber's got away.'

'The one in the cell?'

'No; the one with the money. He stuck up Phil Edison and stole his hat, duster and horse – left him tied up and gagged. The men I had watching the street thought it was Edison leaving town. It took him nearly an hour to get free.'

'I saw that man myself,' the marshal confessed. 'I thought it was Edison too. Did he get a good look at who robbed him?'

'He said he was told not to turn around and makes a point of never arguing with a drawn gun. He was bound and gagged and had a sack put over his head. According to him he didn't see who it was and didn't want to see who it was – figured it was safer that way. I don't blame Edison but I'm starting to feel mighty foolish over this. Not only has the bandit been hiding under my very nose but he gets away with the money as well. We can't track him tonight but I'm taking out a posse at first light,' Braga said. 'Do you feel like a ride?'

'I might as well,' Cleary replied, 'because I have a feeling that you and I are after the same bunch of bad characters.'

Cleary's work often involved periods with little sleep but he had never quite become

30

used to it. The lawman who climbed into his saddle next morning was hardly full of enthusiasm. He joined Braga and a few other horsemen in front of the sheriff's office. Black Baxter was with them sitting grim-faced in the saddle of a tall sorrel horse. He nodded in recognition but said nothing. After a brief exchange of greetings the cavalcade turned their mounts out of town.

The tracks of Edison's pinto showed plainly in the soft dust and the posse was able to follow them at a good pace.

They had been riding for about an hour when Braga pointed to an open area at the side of the trail. 'That's where Josh Baxter disappeared. If you want to look around another minute or two, won't make much difference.'

Cleary said that he would so the party halted. The smell of death hung in the air. 'Something's dead around here,' the marshal said.

'I know, but it ain't Red Baxter,' Braga told him. 'It's one of Juan Diaz's goats. Old Juan grazes his goats all around here. If you look in that ditch over there, you'll see what's left of a black and white goat.'

'Have you asked Diaz if he saw anything?' Cleary enquired.

'No. He's a strange old coot, comes and goes and some reckon he's a few shingles short of a full roof. I wouldn't put too much stock in anything he said, even if we could find him easily. He's been living with and talking to too many goats.'

Aaron Baxter made no effort to explore the scene. He had been there before and by the look on his face, painful memories were coming back. Impatiently he was turning his sorrel down the trail as though in a hurry to leave the area.

The marshal rode about and saw where the bandits had concealed themselves but gained little of value from the site. 'I've seen enough. Let's go.'

They had to canter their mounts to catch up with Baxter who was 200 yards away by then.

An hour later, where the trail led through some pine-covered hills, Cleary suddenly halted them. He pointed to the tracks on the ground. 'We've been fooled,' he announced.

'What makes you think that?' Braga asked.

'The tracks are still there,' Baxter reminded him.

'Sure they are but you can see that the horse is only walking. It's not walking straight like a ridden horse does. You can see where it wandered to the other side of the trail and back again. I think we'll find that pony minus its rider at the next good patch of grass we come to.'

'What about the rider?' Braga asked. He still was not convinced.

'I think he tied the reins up so they wouldn't get in the horse's way and stepped off the horse on to a rock or something beside the trail.'

'But then he'd be on foot,' another man reminded.

'Not if he had a friend waiting with another horse,' Cleary told them. 'I reckon we should start searching back from here.'

Braga and the other posse members were not so sure. The sheriff frowned and shook his head. 'I think we should keep going. Every delay puts the man and the money further away from us.'

Baxter broke his silence again. 'Why would he leave his horse when we were not even close on his heels? He'd be crazy.'

The marshal thought otherwise. 'I'll just check back a bit and if I find nothing I'll catch you up. Chances are that our man's long gone, but if you hear shooting, come running.'

Back tracking was not easy as the posse had ridden over the tracks. Following a hunch, Cleary decided that his time would be better spent looking for a likely place where the bank robber had dismounted. A few minutes later he found what he sought. A large, flat rock about a foot high lay at the side of the trail. Beyond that a sagebrush flat extended to the base of a high rock pillar, a natural landmark that would make a good rendezvous point. Steering the grey around the rock at the trail's edge, he looked between the sage and saw a boot print in the soft, red earth. It seemed a strange place for a hunted man to abandon his horse but the tracks through the sage led straight to the standing rock.

The overnight dew in the shaded prints was beginning to dry out so the marshal knew that his quarry was some hours ahead, but if, for some reason, the man had lingered at the standing rock, he could easily ride into an ambush. A lone man with a much-needed horse was a tempting target for any desperate fugitive. Consequently the lawman kept a sharp eye out for trouble as he neared the red monolith.

Holding a drawn revolver in one hand, he cautiously steered around the rock's base. No sage grew there and the footprints showed clearly. On the other side of the rock, he found his man.

FOUR

The bank robber would cause no further trouble. He was dead, sprawled face-down on the trampled ground, shot twice in the back at close range, his gun still in its holster. The tracks of another man and horse were plain on the ground near the body.

Cleary dismounted and turned over the dead man. The face, even with its shocked expression, was vaguely familiar and he was sure that he had seen the man's picture on a Wanted poster somewhere. The dead man had been taken completely by surprise with no chance to draw his gun. Almost certainly he had known the man who killed him.

The marshal was about to go around the rock and fire signal shots to the posse when he saw movement on a distant hill that was bathed in the bright early morning sunlight. Quickly he took his field-glasses from their case attached to his saddle horn. It took a second or two to locate his target and focus the glasses, but eventually he saw a rider in dark clothes on a dark brown or bay horse.

Detail was hard to distinguish but he thought he could see light-brown saddlebags behind the rider. The only notable features of the horse itself were a pair of white forefeet that showed clearly against the red earth that the animal was walking upon. Steadying the glasses, Cleary checked again but no other details were apparent. It was eerie to be watching from a distance because something sinister seemed to emanate from the tiny figure's presence. Seconds later the rider was over the ridge and gone from sight.

The marshal rode back around the rock and on the trail he saw the posse riding slowly back. They were leading a riderless pinto horse. He raised his six-shooter and fired a shot in the air. The horsemen turned towards him.

'You were right,' Braga was forced to admit when they arrived. 'We found the horse feeding by the roadside. The bridle was off and hanging from the saddle horn. Did you find any tracks?'

'I did and I found the man who made them but he was already dead. He apparently had to meet someone here. Whoever he met killed him and made off with the money.'

The sheriff slapped the heel of his hand to

his forehead. 'Can anything else go wrong?' There was almost a note of despair in his voice.

While leading the others to the body, Cleary said, 'I think I saw the killer. There's a rider a mile or two ahead of us and he's leaving a clear track. I suggest you leave a couple of men on the slower horses here to take the body back to town. The rest of us should get on that rider's trail. We might just run him down.'

For a second the horsemen clustered around the body on the ground and then Braga started barking orders. He delegated three men to collect the body and return it on the pinto horse to Santa Rosa. As he shortened his reins he looked at Black Baxter and the remaining pair of town volunteers. Wheeling his buckskin horse about he said to Cleary, 'Let's get after him.'

The marshal had hoped to take a few short cuts because he knew where the mysterious rider had gone but found his way barred by deep erosion gullies that forced him to make detours. He realized then why the killer had not been as far away as he normally would have been. Negotiating the rough country took time and if their quarry was now in better terrain, he would be increasing his lead considerably.

They reached the ridge where Cleary had last seen the rider and the horse's tracks were plain upon the ground. Another wide flat confronted them. It stretched away to where the rugged mountains rose in the west, their foothills seemingly a mass of dark green pine trees. The posse checked for a moment and looked about. Nothing appeared to be stirring on the mesquite-dotted flat. Then Black Baxter stood in his stirrups and pointed.

In great excitement he called, 'There's dust rising over there. He's probably moving along one of those washouts below the level of the plain.'

The posse swept down off the ridge, each rider taking his own track through the broken ground. They strung out as the more confident riders and more sure-footed horses took the lead. Cleary had no worries about the rough ground. His grey horse was used to it and he knew that it would watch the footing for the pair of them.

Another puff of dust rose ahead of them, not far from where it was first sighted. The idea came to Cleary that their man was not running and could be preparing to give them a hot reception. As they came closer he called to the others, 'Be careful. It don't look like he's running.'

The two lawmen had almost reached the lip of a deep gully when Braga hauled back on his reins. 'It's OK,' he called to Cleary. 'I just heard a bell. It's Juan Diaz and his goats.'

'Watch that he doesn't have company,' the marshal warned.

The pair edged their horses closer and suddenly could see into the deep gully. Huddled together on its floor were an ancient Mexican clad in rags, a small flock of goats, an old dog and a burro carrying a pack. The old man looked up fearfully at the riders but his features relaxed slightly as he recognized Braga. His beard-framed mouth opened in a gap-toothed grin before a frantic rush of Spanish poured forth.

The sheriff spoke quietly to him in the same language, but at first Diaz seemed not to understand. Then in contrast to his enthusiastic greeting, his replies were nervous and he began to stammer.

'He says he's seen the Devil,' Braga translated. 'He's scared stiff.'

'Ask him if he saw the Devil today,' Cleary prompted.

After a long discussion in Spanish, Braga

40

said, 'He reckons the Devil steals his goats and he steals dead children from graveyards. He said he saw him shoot a man today.'

'He probably saw our bank robber getting shot. Ask him what the Devil looked like.'

Another lengthy discussion followed. Diaz seemed to have trouble comprehending but Braga remained calm. Eventually he had enough information to tell Cleary. 'He was a big gringo, all in black, riding a big black stallion with red eyes. The Devil was looking for his goats but could not find them so he killed a man instead and rode away.'

'The description doesn't fit the man I saw. He didn't look all that big, wasn't all in black and his horse was probably a dark bay. As a witness I don't think this man is much use to us. I think we should get on our way again.'

'I agree,' Braga said, as he turned his horse. He shouted a brief farewell to the old man, touched the spurs lightly to his horse's sides and cantered away. The others followed. It took a while to pick up the tracks again but they led steadily westward.

The sheriff began to look worried. 'We should hit the road to Cedar Wells shortly. It gets a fair bit of traffic over it. There's a silver mine in the mountains and ore

41

wagons are going up and down the road regularly. Our man could lose his tracks there. The local bandits use the trick all the time and unfortunately it works well.'

'What's at Cedar Wells?' Cleary enquired.

'Nothing much. It's mostly a supply centre for the mines in the hills and the cattle ranches out along Pentecost Creek. There's a couple of saloons, a general store, a dentist who fills in sometimes as a doctor and a few houses. There are no law officers, but there's no bank either so the place is hardly a target for outlaws.'

They followed a rutted wagon road into the hills. It twisted around the contours of the land and it was almost a surprise when the horsemen rounded a rocky spur and found the town nestled in against a high wall of red rock. Its few buildings had been thrown up in haste with no great effort to build permanent or eye-pleasing structures. Braga explained that it was only in recent times that the Apaches had allowed the miners free access and the latter went to work as quickly as they could before the Indians changed their minds. The Apaches and the miners had never had cordial relations.

A neatly dressed man in his late thirties

42

wearing a clean white shirt, dark trousers and shiny boots was sitting in a chair on the boardwalk reading a newspaper. He lowered it and a friendly smile came to his tanned face.

Upon recognizing the newcomers, he stood up and brushed his dark-brown hair away from his forehead. 'Lou,' he called in a leisurely southern drawl, 'What brings you to our fair city?'

The posse halted and Braga rode over to where the man was by now standing on the edge of the boardwalk. 'I'm looking for a murderer, Doc. We tracked him to the road, but can only guess that he might have come this way. Have you seen any strangers in town?'

Doc replied that he had seen mine workers and teamsters that he did not know but guessed that these would not be the ones that the sheriff sought.

'I get a good view of everyone who enters the town from here,' he said. 'The shadow of the cliff behind makes it too hard to read inside my place so I often sit out here when there's no one needing my services. What does your man look like?'

'He was wearing dark clothes and riding a dark bay or brown horse. We don't have a

43

very good description. An old Mexican goat herder said he was a big gringo in black riding a black stallion with red eyes but I reckon a stranger like that would stand out around here.'

Doc laughed. 'He surely would. I'm sorry to say though, that no such character has ridden in here today.'

Braga introduced Cleary. 'Doc Palmer, meet Tim Cleary, he's a US marshal just helping out temporarily.'

They shook hands. 'A marshal,' Doc said. 'Our local bad boys seem to be attracting a bit of extra attention.'

'Some are,' Cleary said, and left it at that. He did not like talking about current investigations.

'Looks like our man turned the other way where he hit the road and is probably headed for Mexico,' the sheriff admitted. 'We'll get our horses and men fed and will try to figure out where to go from here. I'll see you around, Doc.'

'Sure,' Palmer drawled, as he picked up his newspaper again and settled back in his chair.

Later, with men and horses fed and resting, Braga told Cleary what he intended to do. He would remain in Cedar Wells for a day or two interviewing people and generally making enquiries. He would get a volunteer to stay with him but the others would be free to return to Santa Rosa as most had regular jobs.

'I'll go back with the others,' Cleary said. 'The bank robbery really is not my main purpose. I still have to find those rifles and whoever took them. If I'm not in town when you get back, I'll leave you a letter so you'll know what's going on.'

It was no surprise that Baxter volunteered to remain with the sheriff. He made no secret of the fact that he was still seeking his brother's body and those who had killed him. He hoped that in Cedar Wells he might find some of the answers that had eluded him in Santa Rosa.

FIVE

It was a barking dog that woke Julia. She had no idea of the time but it was still dark. She knew the dog. It belonged to her neighbours and was a sensible animal that only barked when it had a good reason. It might only have been a coyote that had ventured into town as some did occasionally but the girl thought the dog's warning was worth investigating.

She left her bed and walked silently to the window. Partially concealed by the curtains she peered out. At first she saw nothing and then something moved in the shadows on the other side of the road. It was a man and he was keeping close to the wall of the freight barn. Through the window pane she could not hear the footsteps and he seemed to glide along in an eerie silence. As Julia watched the man stepped briefly into a patch of moonlight that he could not avoid. The moonlight shone directly on his face as he looked about and the girl felt the hair rising on the back of her neck. She was sure that she was looking into the face of Josh Baxter. He had worked for Gustavson as long as she had and she knew him well. But it could not be. He was dead. Everyone said so.

Then the man seemed to vanish before her eyes. One second he was there and then the street was empty. Still in disbelief, Julia tried to find an answer for what she had seen. The most logical explanation was that the man had stepped around the corner of the building and was out of sight. Or, had she been dreaming? There was another possibility but she did not want to think about it. Had she seen a ghost?

Daylight came as a relief for she had slept badly. By the time she opened up Gustavson's office, the girl was feeling a little better but she was still troubled by what she had seen during the night. She had intended looking to see if the mysterious visitor had left any tracks but was delayed by customers either delivering goods to be shipped away or collecting goods that the freight wagon had brought in from its last trip to the railhead.

With Black Baxter away and the company's other wagons on the road, Julia was obliged to open the warehouse as well as try

47

to attend to business in the office. She was in no mood for visitors when Cleary came to see her but tried to be pleasant.

'I got in late last night,' the marshal explained. 'Baxter's staying with Braga. He asked me to let you know.'

'I don't know how I'm supposed to run this place on my own, Marshal. I hope you don't want a check of our records or anything complicated like that.'

'Not at this stage, Miss Cross. I don't feel too energetic today. We did a lot of riding yesterday. There was another murder and we were supposed to be chasing the Devil. No doubt Black Baxter will tell you about it when he comes back but I have to get back to Uncle Sam's business.'

On impulse Julia asked, 'Do you believe in the supernatural, Marshal Cleary?'

The lawman thought for a while. 'Maybe,' he answered. 'Folks say there's something to it but I can't say I've had any experiences in that area. Why do you ask?'

'Because last night I looked out of my window. The house I rent is just over the road from here. I'm sure I saw Josh Baxter on the other side of the road, in front of the freight office. Josh is supposed to be dead; I'm wondering if I saw a ghost.'

Cleary frowned. The problems in Santa Rosa had been complicated enough just with human activity. Now it seemed that devils and ghosts were becoming involved. But he knew that the devil story was false and strongly suspected that the girl had not seen a ghost either. 'I could be wrong,' he said at length, 'but I don't think you saw a ghost. Miss Cross, Red Baxter might not be dead. No body has ever been found.'

'But Josh was a happy-go-lucky, likeable sort of person. Why would he want to disappear?'

'I don't know. Keep quiet about this and let's see what else develops. Do you know if Red Baxter had any problems with anyone?'

Julia looked about as if to ensure that no one else was in earshot. 'I heard that he was in trouble with Phil Edison, the gambler. He never said anything about it and I wouldn't ask, but word around town was that he lost a lot of money gambling with Edison and couldn't pay up. Edison swore that one way or another, Josh would pay. It might only be a rumour but that's what I heard.'

'That gives a reason for Red Baxter to disappear, but it doesn't give him a reason to steal those guns and also the mules. They are things that a man would find hard to sell unless he already had a market lined up. But I suppose he could have done that. He would have met a lot of people travelling to and from the railhead.'

Any further discussion was cut short by the sound of someone running along the boardwalk. Cleary turned in time to see a red-faced, panting townsman come through the door. 'Marshal,' he gasped, as he sought to get his breath. 'There's been two killings up at the sheriff's office – Doc Hadlow just found 'em – went there to change the prisoner's dressing – Found Marvin Wilkes and the prisoner both shot – blood everywhere.'

Cleary turned to go. 'Remember what I said. Don't say anything about what you saw.' He was gone even before Julia could nod in agreement.

A crowd was already gathering and Cleary had to elbow his way through them to get in the door. Doctor Hadlow, his lined face a picture of frustration was trying to keep onlookers away from the scene. Already some had trodden in the large bloodstain near the body of Wilkes.

'Everyone out,' Cleary ordered and reinforced the instruction by catching an on-looker by the shoulders and propelling him out of the door. The others grumbled but followed. The marshal slammed and locked the door behind them. 'Can you tell what happened?' he asked.

In a tired voice Hadlow told him. 'Marvin wasn't shot, he was stabbed in the heart as he opened the office door. I found the prisoner off the bunk at the front of his cell – probably thought his friends were there to rescue him. Instead, someone shot him.'

Cleary picked up a coat that was on the floor in front of the cell. It had been powder burnt and had holes through it in a couple of places. 'Looks like the killer wrapped this coat around his gun hand to muffle the sound. If that coat was Braga's he's going to need a new one. How many times was the prisoner shot?'

'Only once. The killer was at close range and put the bullet right through his victim's heart. It must have been one of the outlaws, but why would they kill one of their own?'

'It was to stop him talking. He was too badly wounded to get out of jail so they shot him. These characters are completely ruthless. Did he ever say anything to you?'

'Very little and then it was only to do with his bullet wound. Sometimes he pretended to be semi-conscious to avoid being questioned by Braga.'

'Lou's not going to be happy when he sees what's happened here. First the bandits get away with the bank's money and now he's lost a prisoner and a good man has been murdered as well. The man we chased was murdered too. An old Mexican told us he was killed by the Devil and considering the amount of spilled blood lately, he might not have been far wrong. I'll make some notes and the sheriff will want a statement from you, Doc. Then we'll get the undertaker to collect the bodies and arrange for someone to clean this place up.'

Some hours later Cleary was feeding his horse in the small corral behind the sheriff's office. He always found it relaxing listening to the animal's rhythmic chewing and for a short while he seemed to forget the pressures of the day. On more than one occasion a good idea would come into his head during these quiet times and that day was one such occasion. Due to the morning's excitement he had almost forgotten about Edison, the gambler. He needed to know more about him. There was the connection with Red Baxter and a suspicion that the distinctive clothes and horse might have been a ruse to allow the bank robber to escape.

Hoping that the gambler had not left town, the marshal hurried to the livery stable. To his relief, he saw the pinto horse still in a stall. His next stop was at the closest of the town's two saloons. He found Edison there.

The gambler was seated alone with a deck of cards before him and a glass of whiskey in his hand. His black suit looked slightly rumpled and the butt of a revolver showed where the coat had been pushed back on the right side.

As he approached, Cleary saw that the gun butt pointed forward for a left-handed cross draw or a military-style, right-handed draw still favoured by some former soldiers and professional gamblers. The arrangement offered the option of either hand being used and was convenient for a man seated in a chair. He wondered if Edison was left-handed.

The gambler regarded the lawman coolly as he watched him approach. 'You look like you're on business,' he greeted. 'Have a seat.

As you can see, business is kind of slow today. Are you sure that I could not inveigle you into a game of chance?'

'I'm sure. I'm the world's worst poker player. I won't beat around the bush. As you know, I'm investigating Red Baxter's disappearance and the theft of military rifles. I have heard that you have threatened Baxter. Is that right?'

'You heard right. Red thought he was a champion poker player but he wasn't. I accepted his IOUs for three hundred dollars but then he welshed on the deal and claimed that I had cheated. In my profession I cannot afford to be labelled a cheat. One thing led to another and I ended up telling Baxter that the next time we met he had better be wearing a gun.'

'Were you prepared to kill him?'

Edison took another sip of his drink and thought for a second or two. 'Not really,' he finally admitted. 'Not unless he tried to kill me. I'm a gambler and sometimes I operate on bluff. I actually stayed away from Santa Rosa to avoid a confrontation, but with Baxter dead, I decided to resume my regular beat again. Everyone liked Red, but he was a very weak man and far from the upright citizen he pretended to be. Lou Braga does not like people shooting in his town and I did not want to be barred from it for shooting Baxter even in self-defence. I know that I won't see my three hundred dollars again but was not sorry to hear that he had been killed. He had created a very awkward situation for me. However, I assure you that I had nothing to do with Baxter's death.'

'You're sure he is dead?'

Edison took another sip of his drink. 'That seems the most likely possibility.'

Cleary then switched his line of questioning and asked the circumstances regarding the theft by the bank robber of Edison's clothing and horse. But the gambler stuck to his story. He insisted that he did not know the man because he had never seen him. The voice, too, was unfamiliar. He had obeyed the gunman's instructions and allowed himself to be tied up because he knew never to argue with a drawn gun. 'I make my living by calculating the odds,' Edison explained. 'In risky situations, I prefer not to take chances.'

Cleary rose from his chair. 'Thanks for the help. I'll ask you to stay around until Sheriff Braga gets back. He'll probably want a word with you.'

'I won't be leaving. This Saturday is payday for the ranches and miners around here and there will be some ripe pigeons ready for plucking. I'll see you around.'

You sure will, Cleary said to himself, as he walked away.

SIX

Braga arrived back at Santa Rosa tired and feeling that he had wasted his time. When he heard the latest news, he almost despaired. Regardless of his best efforts whatever small degree of control he had over matters was slipping away. He had heard all the reports of the killings and was sitting, shoulders slumped over his desk when Cleary walked into the office.

'Could you stand a drink after such a rough homecoming?' the marshal asked.

Braga shrugged his shoulders. 'Why not? There's not much else can go wrong. I may as well be drunk as the way I am.'

Cleary produced a small flask of whiskey from the side pocket of his coat. The sheriff found a couple of rather dusty glasses in a wall cupboard, blew the dust out of them and set them on the desk. The marshal sloshed a generous amount into each glass.

'Here's luck,' Braga said, as he raised his drink. He took a sip and shuddered. 'We'll need luck to survive this stuff. What's in it?'

'I think we'd be happier not knowing, but over at the local saloon they're calling it whiskey,' Cleary replied. 'Now let's get our heads together and see what we can make of all this mess.'

'You are right about the mess. There are a lot of unhappy people around here at present. The town council does not approve of a couple of murders, the bank manager is getting a bit narrow-minded about the robbery, Uncle Sam doesn't like losing his guns, Gustavson is a bit peeved about his stolen mule team and Black Baxter is rather keen to find out what happened to Red. We don't need to look far for unhappy customers.'

'What about suspects?' Cleary asked, after regaining the breath taken away by his first mouthful.

Braga had another sip and this time hardly grimaced. 'I reckon Phil Edison needs watching. His turning up proved vital to the bank robber's escape. His fancy talk could be similar to the gang leader.'

'I agree,' said Cleary, 'but he was in town when that bank robber was murdered out in the desert. He couldn't be the one that Diaz called the Devil. I think he needs watching though.' He paused and then continued, 'We can't write Red Baxter out of this deal

58

either. The theft of those rifles could have been an inside job. What if Baxter's still alive?'

'I've wondered about that myself but still think it unlikely. Black Baxter would also be in a position to know about those guns but he would hardly have his own brother murdered.'

'There's one more person could be involved,' the marshal said tentatively. 'I have no reason to believe she is, but Julia Cross is in a position to pass on information about valuable freight.'

Braga shook his head in disbelief. 'Not Julia. She's as honest as they come.'

Cleary smiled. 'You wouldn't be in love with her, would you?'

'The whole damn town's in love with her. We all think she's great. But for your information I'm engaged to a very nice girl who lives out of town on a ranch. She would shoot me quick if I ever looked sideways at Julia.'

'Of course, the lady herself might not know that she is supplying information to the wrong side. Some crooks are very good at getting information out of unsuspecting people just in casual conversation.'

'Julia's a bit too smart for that,' Braga

assured him.

Juan Diaz saw the Devil again on the following morning. He lay atop a mesa concealed by a screen of greasewood. Though the distant rider was but a tiny speck on the flat below, there was something that he recognized and fear seized him like a cold hand on the back of his neck. Cringing down, the old man stared as though hypnotized and prayed that the sinister figure would not look in his direction. A normal man could not possibly detect him but with the Devil anything was possible.

Far below, Diaz saw other movement. The Devil was halted by a high, pale-coloured rock. Was he waiting to waylay the approaching rider? Then another pair of riders appeared and Diaz began to tremble. He knew then that the Devil was assembling his men. Were they coming after his goats again? Muttering to himself again, the old man retreated to where he had left his animals. Three of his goats had bells around their necks and he caught these in turn and tied the bell clappers so they could not ring. Then, with a curt order to the dog, he sent it behind the goats and started them walking toward Santa Rosa. He did not like

60

towns or people, but Sheriff Braga was his friend. He would protect him.

Carl Gustavson shifted uncomfortably on the hard seat of the mud wagon that provided a weekly passenger and mail service between Santa Rosa and Joshua Flats. He was a giant of a man, well over six feet with massive shoulders. Sixty years, most of them on the frontier, had put a fair bit of silver into his flaxen hair and beard and added a few extra pounds to his waistline but he was still an imposing figure in any company. 'You ought to pad the seats in this contraption,' he shouted to the driver.

Henry Reckitt, the wizened driver, spat tobacco juice over the side, shifted the reins of the six-mule team to one hand and twisted around. 'You're gettin' too fussy in your old age, Carl. Just think back on the times before you made your pile. You'd figure yourself lucky to be gettin' a ride like this.'

Ralph Hutchens, Gustavson's newly hired mule-skinner, threw in his opinion. 'This wagon mightn't be as comfortable as a coach but it beats hell out of walking.'

'That's right,' Reckitt agreed. 'Carl, it don't seem all that long ago that you came ploddin' into Santa Rosa draggin' your whip in the dust beside an ox team with the seat hangin' out of your pants.'

'That was twenty years ago, Henry,' Gustavson laughed. 'Shows how old we're both getting.'

Hutchens stopped any further reminiscing. 'There's riders coming in from over here on the right.' As the others looked in the direction indicated, he said in alarm, 'They're wearing masks – they're road agents.'

Gustavson swore but Reckitt took more positive action. He started to whip up his mules.

Hutchens half drew his sixgun. 'There's four of them. Can we hold them off?'

'Forget that idea,' Gustavson said firmly. He turned to the driver. 'Best save your mules, Henry. We can't outrun them. They only have to shoot one of the leaders and they could bring down the whole team. Lives are the only things that can't be replaced. Slow down, Henry. If nobody does anything stupid we'll probably only get robbed.'

Reckitt eased back the team and glanced over his shoulder at the approaching horsemen. 'I sure hope you're right, Carl.'

Very deliberately, Hutchens unbuckled his gunbelt and placed it with its holstered revolver on the floor of the wagon and moved away from it. 'I want them to see that I ain't armed,' he explained. 'They'll be less likely to get itchy trigger fingers then.'

SEVEN

The masked riders overtook the mud wagon and came up on both sides of it. 'Pull up,' the leading bandit said and reinforced the order by pointing a long-barrelled Colt at the driver. 'I'll kill anyone who touches a gun.'

'Nobody's going to resist,' Gustavson said. 'There's a gun in my coat pocket but I'm not fool enough to try and use it.'

'You're being smart, Gustavson,' the bandit said as Reckitt hauled back on the reins and jammed his foot on the brake. 'Now I want the three of you out of the wagon on this side. Don't try any tricks.'

The three men alighted and stood side by side with their arms raised. None looked very happy, Gustavson the least of all. He had been collecting a few accounts from regular clients and had nearly a thousand dollars in cash in his bag. But he was reconciled to losing it in the interests of staying alive.

Nodding toward a bandit with a floppy

black hat pulled low over his forehead, the leader snapped, 'Get their guns and any cash.'

The man dismounted quickly. 'Where are your guns?' he demanded.

Reckitt turned his right hip slightly and the man pushed a gun barrel into his chest as he plucked the driver's revolver from its holster and threw it away.

Next it was Gustavson's turn. 'My gun's in the left, inside pocket of my coat,' the big freighter said. Then his eyes widened and he opened his mouth as if to speak again.

But if he spoke at all the words were drowned out by the roar of the bandit's gun. Fired from a range of less than six inches, the bullet tore through the big man's heart and dropped him face-down on the dusty ground.

The other prisoners cried out in shock and looked about to take to their heels. 'Stand still and you won't be shot,' the outlaw leader barked. When the pair were standing like statues, he turned to the killer. 'Why the hell did you do that?'

'Had to,' came the grunted reply.

'Search him for his wallet and check this other *hombre* for a gun.'

Hutchens said urgently. 'My gun's over

there in the coach – I ain't carrying any weapons.'

Turning to another rider on a bay horse, the bandit leader ordered, 'Get the mail bags and go through Gustavson's bag.'

'You shouldn't be takin' them letters,' Reckitt had recovered sufficiently from his shock to warn. 'There's no money in them.'

'Shut your mouth, or join Gustavson on the ground. I know that sometimes people put money in letters and if anyone is sending instructions to your local lawman we like to know what's being said. If we let you go, I don't want you saying too much about us – no detailed descriptions or anything helpful to the law.'

Hutchens said nervously, 'We can't describe you anyway. We can only see your eyes above those bandannas.'

'You're learning. Now stand still, the pair of you. The better you behave, the sooner we'll be on the way.'

Cleary called at the freight depot. Baxter was busy arranging boxes and barrels in the shed and checking them against a handwritten list that he had. The lawman gave him a wave and went into the office.

Julia was busy at her desk sorting waybills

66

and accounts into various piles. 'I won't be long,' she called when she saw Cleary. 'Mr Gustavson's coming home today and I want to have everything up-to-date.'

The marshal glanced idly around the office and his eye fell on a framed photograph of Gustavson and his staff in front of the warehouse. Being the only woman Julia was easy to identify and among the others he easily picked out the two Baxters. They were remarkably alike and because the photograph did not differentiate between their hair colouring, even though he knew Black Baxter, he was not sure which one he was. 'Those Baxters are alike,' he observed.

Julia agreed as she arranged the papers on her desk. 'If Josh didn't have red hair, he could easily be mistaken for Aaron. That's why people called them Red and Black instead of their real names. They were very close and poor Aaron has not been himself since Josh disappeared.'

'What can you tell me about Red Baxter and the money he owes to Phil Edison?'

'Only what I told you before, I heard a rumour that Josh had lost a lot of money gambling and his life had been threatened, but I don't know any other details and don't want to know.'

'It appears to me that Josh had a good reason to disappear and the sale of those rifles and the mule team would give him a good stake to start somewhere else.'

The girl frowned. 'Mr Gustavson thought of that too but then he reckoned that Josh would not have the criminal connections necessary to sell the mules and guns quickly.'

'It's a good point,' Cleary admitted. 'How long were the rifles in the warehouse before they were shipped out?'

'A couple of days. We wait till we get a full wagonload before things are freighted out. Even if Josh was that way inclined, I doubt he would have had time to organize any illegal sales.'

The urgent beating of hoofs outside stopped any further discussion. Nobody rode through town like that without a good reason. A cowhand on a foam-covered black horse came spurring past the freight office.

'Looks like he's headed for Braga's office. I'd better go,' Cleary said.

He ran along the boardwalk and saw the rider jump from his horse and run into the sheriff's office. The horse stood where it was, head lowered, sides heaving and sweat dripping from it on to the ground.

Braga was walking urgently to the rider when Cleary arrived. Still panting from his exertions the young cowhand told how Reckitt had driven the mail wagon to the ranch where he worked. The mail had been stolen by four bandits and Carl Gustavson murdered in cold blood.

'If they've interfered with the mail,' Cleary said, 'it's a federal offence so now I'm involved in this latest mess too.'

Braga allowed himself a quick smile. 'That's good. I could do with some professional help.' He fished a silver dollar from his pants pocket. 'I'll toss you to see who breaks the news to Julia. She was very fond of Gustavson. She'll take it hard.'

Cleary won the toss and decided that Braga could be the one to break the news. 'When you get back,' he said, 'let's get riding. We might be able to recruit a couple of posse men from the ranch hands. The trail's hot so let's get on it as quick as we can. I'll start getting our horses ready while you're breaking the news.'

Reluctantly, Braga headed for the door. He paused and looked back. 'Are you sure you don't want to see Julia?'

'Not under these circumstances, besides, she knows you better. I'm not much good at breaking sad news.'

'Who is?' Braga asked over his shoulder as he left the office.

EIGHT

The two lawmen set out for Compton's Spade Ranch where the survivors of the hold-up were waiting with Gustavson's body. They moved along at a smart pace but did not exert their horses unduly as both anticipated that it would be a long hunt for the bandits.

As they rode, Braga described how badly Julia and Baxter had taken the news of their boss's murder. But for once, Baxter was not keen to join the hunt for the killers. He said that Julia would need a hand with business arrangements and with notifying Gustavson's immediate family who were in nearby towns. The dead man's wife had died several years before. 'Julia is sure going to be busy for a while,' the sheriff said. Then a thought struck him. 'I was meaning to tell you when I got the chance that I might have found a name for Diaz's Devil. Doc Palmer remembered there was a fancy-talking *hombre* named Bennett who used to work at the Cedar Wells mine. Apparently Bennett left his job over a year ago and as far as folks knew, had gone elsewhere. According to Doc, Bennett showed up at his place about a month ago early one morning. It seems he had a bad tooth that Doc had to take out. He didn't say much and Doc didn't ask much, but by the look of his clothes, Bennett had come into money after leaving the job at the mine. Doc figured that Bennett was still living somewhere in the area otherwise he would not have been looking for a dentist at Cedar Wells. His chances would be better in a bigger town. I checked with the mine records. There was a Sydney Bennett who worked there for about a year. He seemed to be well educated and spoke very correctly. Otherwise he was described as fairly average, probably in his thirties. That was about all folks remembered about him.'

'Bennett might not be our man,' Cleary said, 'but at least we have a name to investigate.'

The rancher, Herb Compton, was eagerly awaiting the lawmen. He was a wiry little man with a bald head, somewhere in his fifties. A six-shooter was belted around his waist and the cartridge belt filled with shiny new cartridges. 'When you're ready to go, Lou, I'll go with you with a couple of my men,' he said.

Braga introduced Cleary, but said that he would like to interview the witnesses to the murder before departing from the ranch. He had arranged for the Santa Rosa undertaker to come out and collect the body.

While Compton waited impatiently, the two lawmen interviewed Reckitt and Hutchens. Both men could only give general descriptions but confirmed that the leader seemed to be well spoken. They mentioned, too, that the killers seemed to know Gustavson and might even have been expecting him.

'Why do you think he was killed?' Cleary asked.

Hutchens scratched his head and thought for a while. 'I can't say for sure – could be he recognized the road agent.'

'The boss bandit got caught by surprise,' Reckitt added. 'He asked that other coyote why he did it. He just said that he had to.'

'So the killing wasn't planned,' Cleary said. 'Was there anything about the bandit that Gustavson would be able to recognize?'

Reckitt answered, 'Ain't likely. We could only see their eyes and the one that shot Carl had his hat pulled down real low.'

When the lawmen had learned as much as they could, they mounted their horses and with Compton and his men, rode to the scene of the robbery. They learned little from the tracks and were about to start their pursuit when Diaz appeared from the brush. Like a strange animated scarecrow he hurried toward them calling out in Spanish as he came.

'Crazy old galoot,' Compton muttered under his breath.

The old man tottered up to Braga, the only person he really trusted and a stream of stammering words poured from his lips while his arms kept pointing to the hills in the west.

With great patience, the sheriff listened. Sometimes he would interrupt and ask a question as he tried to make sense of what he was hearing. Finally he said to the others, 'Diaz has seen the Devil and his men again. He saw them gathering yesterday in a place where he has seen them before. This morning he saw them again at a different place. They had a fire going. He knows that they were going to cook him and his goats so he's heading for town.'

'Crazy as a loon,' Compton muttered.

'I'm not so sure,' Cleary said. 'Can he tell us where he saw these things?'

'He already has. He saw the Devil meeting

his men at a big pale rock that's in a valley beyond those hills. Reckons he's seen them meeting there before. Seems they have regular get-togethers there.'

One of Compton's men, Ned Jocelyn, announced, 'I reckon I know the place he's talking about. That rock's a different colour to all the others: there's no mistaking it.'

'Where were they lighting their fire?' Cleary asked. He was a little surprised that the bandits would risk betraying their presence with a fire.

Braga translated the question and after much babbling and wild gesticulation, the answer came. 'He reckons they were about three miles to the south in an arroyo where there are a lot of Joshua trees.'

Compton nodded in agreement. 'I reckon I know the place. We've had trouble getting cattle out of the brush there.'

Braga translated again. 'Diaz has changed his mind about going to town and now wants to know if he can move his goats on to your ranch and camp there until we run down the Devil.'

'I guess so, but tell him I don't want them goats around the ranch house. Tell the poor old sonofagun that my men will keep the Devil away.'

'How do you think we should play this?' Braga asked, as he gathered up his reins.

'Let's head for where Diaz reckoned the Devil and his boys had their fire,' Cleary replied.

'You're taking a risk on the word of a crazy man,' Compton warned.

'I know that. But if he's right, we've saved ourselves a lot of tracking and will be a lot closer to our men than if we had to trail them from the scene of the killing.'

Compton led the way setting a lively pace over the red, stony ridges, weaving through the tall cactus plants that grew profusely there. They halted for a few minutes to rest the horses on the crest of a particularly steep hill and the rancher pointed to a dark mass of trees about half a mile below them. From a distance they looked like a solid mass of spiky, green foliage. He pointed to the bare red soil of an arroyo that cut through the Joshuas like a scar. 'If the Devil's down there, I reckon he would have followed that arroyo. It's just too hard riding through the brush.'

They descended the slope and were soon weaving their way between the spiky trees. There were game trails but animals were lower than mounted men so the riders were scratched as they pushed through the sharp foliage. All were greatly relieved when Compton finally led them to clear ground where flood waters had gouged a path.

The rancher slid his horse down the bank to what occasionally was a stream bed. 'I reckon they stopped somewhere along here if Diaz can be believed. It's best if we turn down the arroyo because the country is even worse on its upper reaches.'

'Makes sense,' Cleary agreed. 'Lead on.'

They had not travelled far when Compton pointed to something white caught in the brush. On closer examination it was a small piece of paper with a charred edge. A short distance away there were similar fragments caught in various bushes.

'Diaz was right,' Braga said. 'Looks like there's been a fire around here somewhere. I think they might have been burning the mail after they robbed it. These little bits have probably been carried away on the wind.'

Around a bend in the old stream bed, they saw the remains of a fire.

'Everyone keep back,' Cleary warned as he dismounted. 'I want to examine any signs they left.'

'I ain't sure you'll learn much from them,' Compton muttered. 'You'll probably only see where a few men tied up their horses and burned the mail.'

'But we might find a trail to follow,' Braga reminded him.

Cleary dropped his horse's reins on the ground so that it would stand and then advanced carefully to study the scene. He found a heap of ashes and burnt paper and a canvas mail bag that had been slashed open. Anger rose inside him for he knew how precious letters were to people in isolated communities.

Four men had left their tracks in the sandy soil and by the number of cigarette butts scattered about, the gang had taken their time in plundering the mail. The lawman checked where the horses had been tied but only found an empty whiskey bottle that the riders had discarded. The whiskey had been a common brand so nothing was learned from the discovery. Cleary called in the others and they muttered angrily at the sight of the burned mail.

'A lot of folks' lives are affected by what comes in the mail,' Compton growled. 'It's a pretty low sort of a skunk that destroys letters like that.'

'No one ever reckoned these sonsabitches was high-grade skunks,' Jocelyn reminded him sourly.

The posse mounted and moved on following the plainly visible trail left by the bandits' horses. The country changed gradually and eventually the posse moved into terrain where the brush was not so thick. In places the soft ground gave way to wide expanses of bare rock and tracking became difficult. Occasionally an iron shoe marked some of the rock but tracking was both slow and arduous.

Compton swore under his breath. 'They're heading for Mustang Creek. The stream flows mostly over bare rock and I suspect they'll ride up or down the creek and emerge on a slab of rock somewhere where they won't leave a track. We'll have hell's own job trying to follow them.'

The rancher's prediction proved to be accurate. They could trace the killers to the stream but their tracks did not emerge on the other side.

After some discussion with Compton, the lawmen decided that they would ride upstream as downstream led out into ranches and country where the outlaws were likely to be seen. They rode in single file watching both sides of the creek but could see no sign of their quarry.

About a mile along the streambed they reached a point where a thick growth of willows made a wall of light green foliage that reached right to the water. Cleary checked his horse and looked around. 'I reckon they came out of the creek through these willows.'

'Don't look like it to me,' murmured Compton. 'Horses going through there would break branches and things.

The marshal disagreed. 'Green willows are nice and springy. You can push them out of the way and they spring back without breaking. But the leaves get twisted around. If you look you can see the undersides of the leaves on that tree over there. Too many are showing for it to be just a trick of the wind. I think that's where our men have left the creek.'

Cleary led the way pushing through the trees. Just at the water's edge there was a patch of mud and a hoofprint showed clearly in the middle of it. 'They went through here,' he called.

Tracking was difficult but the searchers concentrated on the area where travelling was easiest for horses and picked up enough tracks to keep them heading in the right general direction. When they reached an open area of barren red earth, the marshal cursed under his breath as he saw the hoofprints crossing it. 'They've fooled us,' he said.

NINE

The tracks were plain to see. They were left by a single horse. One rider had acted as a decoy.

'What do we do now?' Compton asked.

'The rest of the gang have gained quite a long start on us now,' Braga said. 'But I think we should go back to the creek and try again.'

'Makes sense to me,' Compton said.

Cleary did not agree. 'I might be wrong,' he told them. 'But I think that is exactly what the decoy expects us to do. He could have ridden around that bare patch but he wanted us to see that we have been fooled. He expects us to turn back and my guess is that he won't be anywhere near as careful from now on. Let's try for the bird in the hand rather than the three in the bush.'

Braga looked doubtful but was prepared to compromise. 'What if we try to follow up these tracks for a mile or so? If he's still hiding them, we can turn back but if he's grown over-confident, we'll follow him up.'

Compton consulted with his two cow-hands who knew the area from round-ups. Hatton, a silent, older man, finally broke his silence. 'The tracking will get easier as we get out of this rocky country. Let's go along with the marshal's idea. It's better to get one than miss them all.'

The decoy rider had become careless. That much was obvious. He was so sure that the posse would turn back that he made little effort to conceal his tracks. As Hatton had predicted, the trail led over a rocky ridge to a widely grassed area where cattle were feeding in small groups. They scattered as the riders approached.

'They'll give you some hard times getting those critters out of the brush at the next round-up,' Braga told the rancher.

'They always do but I put my best men and horses into this area. We don't leave too many behind. Last round-up though, we had some trouble here for a while. It was a new feller called Syd Bennett. His horse fell with him but got up first and got away. He had knotted his reins together and they didn't fall under the horse's feet and stop it like they was supposed to. One of the men saw the loose horse and we had to go searching for Bennett. Some of the smarter cows doubled back into the brush again so we had a lot of extra work. Bennett hisself was a bit scratched up but wasn't really hurt.'

The name struck a chord with both lawmen.

'Does Bennett still work for you?' Braga asked.

'No. I only took him on for the round-up.'

Cleary asked, 'Do you know where he went?'

'No. He's a drifter. He was a fair hand – came from back East somewhere. Spoke like he had a good education, for all the good it did him. It didn't teach him that knottin' his reins together might have been all right in the East but it wasn't a smart trick for brush-poppin'.'

'What did he look like?' A note of eagerness had crept into Cleary's voice.

Compton screwed up his face and thought a while. 'I reckon he'd be in his early thirties. He had brown hair, was probably a bit taller than average and had a slight build. He had a short beard when he worked for me but likely shaved it off later. There was nothing special about him except the way he talked.'

Braga asked, 'So he's not around these parts now?'

The rancher shrugged. 'He could be. I don't get away from the ranch very often and don't see a lot of people, but I don't think he's working for any of the neighbouring ranches. Why the big interest in him?'

'His name was suggested as the leader of the men we're chasing,' Cleary said. 'We have no evidence that he is but we have to follow up anything that might lead us to Diaz's Devil.'

Jocelyn stood in his stirrups and pointed. 'There's cattle coming our way.'

A long string of cattle could be seen moving across a distant clearing. They were trotting along led by a large red and white steer with massive horns.

'Something's scared them,' Compton observed. 'They're moving away from good feed and water.'

Hatton said, 'Just over that rise is a soak and some cattle water there in preference to walking all the way to the creek and back to where they feed. There's good feed around the soak and they only move away if there are people about. I reckon our decoy might be setting up camp there.'

'We might be lucky,' Braga told the others. 'The gang might think that they've thrown us off and might have come together again.'

85

Cleary turned his grey to the side. 'Let's get out of the way of those cattle. We don't want them turning back and warning who-ever is at the soak.'

The posse kept under cover as much as possible, riding to a point in the brush where they would not be seen by the already spooked cattle. There they waited until the stock had all passed them.

Webster 'Weasel' Andrews was more annoyed than worried. He should have been many miles ahead of any posse, but instead he was lying in the shade near the soak with his hobbled horse nearby. At a most in-convenient time an old bullet wound in his hip had started giving trouble. Increasing pain had forced him to ride slower and slower and upon reaching the soak, he decided to rest for the night or at least until the pain had eased. A veteran outlaw, he was almost certain that he had frustrated any pursuers. They would realize that they had been led away from their main purpose and he imagined them riding hard back to the creek in an attempt to make up for lost time. Less observant lawmen might not have seen where he left the creek, in which case he need not worry at all. If his hip had not been aching so much he would have allowed himself a smile at the thought of the posse trying to follow the others with night falling.

Weasel was stretched out on the grass in the shade and the pain seemed to be subsiding. Drowsiness was creeping upon him and he made no effort to fight it until his horse snorted.

Instantly he was awake and came to a sitting position, reaching for his gun as he did so. The horse was standing with head high and ears pricked, looking back the way he had come. Years of dodging the law had honed his instinct for survival. He looked in the same direction as the horse and could see nothing amiss but that was not reassuring. The horse was still tense and watchful with its nostrils distended to catch any scents that the breeze might carry.

The mesquite and cactus surrounding the soak concealed it from distant view but it also prevented him from seeing who or what was approaching. Then a twig cracked and in the strained silence it sounded like a gunshot. He reckoned there were at least two men nearby but clung to hope that they might not have seen him because he was at ground level and could have been screened by the surrounding bushes.

'Don't move – drop the gun.' A voice came

from the nearby brush. At the same time a man appeared in a position to cut him off from his horse. Footsteps in the trees behind him betrayed the presence of another man. He was covered on three sides.

Because of a number of outstanding murder charges against him, Weasel Andrews knew that any surrender would only lead to the hangman's rope, so he decided to go out fighting. Forgetting his injured hip, he bounded to his feet and charged the nearest posse man that he could see.

Cleary saw him rushing toward him and saw the muzzle of the outlaw's big Remington .44 swinging in his direction. He fired a fraction of a second before Andrews. It was a comparatively easy shot for a man who was ready. The outlaw, with a bullet in his chest was on his way to the ground before he squeezed the trigger and his own shot went skywards.

'Drop your gun!' Cleary called urgently. He did not want to kill the man.

The fallen man defiantly muttered something in reply, but his words were drowned out by a shot and his body was punched back violently on to the ground. The revolver fell from his grasp. Compton raised his rifle for another shot.

'Stop shooting,' Braga called as he saw Cleary rush forward to the stricken man.

Andrews was struggling convulsively on the ground and making choking sounds. Even as the marshal knelt beside him, the prostrate man twitched and went still.

'Damnit,' Cleary muttered angrily. 'We needed him alive but he didn't give us much choice.' He looked closer at the dark-haired man's small pinched features. 'I know this one. He is, or was, Weasel Andrews. No wonder he didn't want to be taken alive. He would not have talked even if he could have. The law's been after this *hombre* for three years.'

Braga joined them. 'Let's go through his stuff and see if we can find anything that might link him to someone else.'

Andrews' belongings were few but they did find a large silver watch inscribed with the name, J.E. Hopkins.

Braga examined the watch and sighed with relief. 'At least we know that we haven't shot an innocent man. Jordan Hopkins had his watch stolen in a stage hold-up about six weeks ago.'

The dead outlaw's saddle-bags yielded up a bundle of notes of various denominations and nearly twenty dollars in coins. Cleary counted it and noted the amount in his notebook.

Hatton's eyes narrowed as he saw the pile of money. A crafty look crossed his whiskered face. 'There's only us five here knows about this money,' he said in a conspiratorial tone. 'We could split it up an' not a soul would be any the wiser.'

'I would,' Cleary growled, 'and Lou would as well. We like to sleep nights, so get any notions like that right out of your head.'

'Just joking,' Hatton said sheepishly although it was obvious that he had not been.

'What happens now?' Compton asked.

The marshal looked at the low sun and lengthening shadows. 'We'll camp here tonight and next morning take Andrews to a place more accessible to a wagon and plant him. In the unlikely event that relatives want to claim his body, they'll be able to find it.'

'Weasel was only wanted by lawmen when he was alive,' Braga said. 'It's unlikely anyone wants his carcass now. They can't eat him, his hide's no good and his head on a wall wouldn't do a damn thing for the decorations.'

TEN

The dog was barking again. Julia was unsure of the time but her curiosity was aroused. She slipped out of bed and hurried to the window. Taking care to remain hidden she peered out. A short while later she saw the figure of a man moving past her house. The moonlight was not as strong as the previous time but the form resembled that of Josh Baxter. Once the man stopped and she saw the pale gleam of a face that was turned toward her. He could not see her but it was as though he sensed he was being observed. Then he hurried away and disappeared around the corner of the alley. Now all thoughts of a supernatural being were gone. This was a living man. Quickly donning a robe and slippers, the girl removed a small revolver from a drawer in her dressing table, placed it in the pocket of her robe. She was not sure that she could shoot anyone, but the weapon was a comforting weight in her pocket as she moved to the front door.

The door opened silently and Julia kept in

the shadows as she crept on to the porch. A familiar sound came to her ears – the clinking of a chain. It was not the eerie clanking of chains said to be associated with some ghosts but a sound that she heard several times each working day. Someone was opening the chain that secured the doors of the Gustavson freight warehouse. The doors could not be seen from her house because the office was directly in front of them but the sound carried in the night stillness. The nocturnal visitor was entering the warehouse and using a key to do it.

Aaron Baxter had one key and she had a duplicate in the office safe. She remembered then that there was a second lock on the chain and only Carl Gustavson possessed the key. This arrangement had enabled him to enter the warehouse at times when the staff were not working. If it was not Aaron Baxter unlocking the chain, it could only be someone with Gustavson's key and that would have been taken from his dead body.

But discovering the intruder was one thing and doing something about it would not be a simple proposition. With both lawmen hunting the bandits and Black Baxter living some distance away, Julia had no one upon whom she could rely for help. She was no coward, but knew that it would be extremely foolish to confront the intruder alone. As quietly as she could, she slipped across the street and peered down the alleyway that led to the warehouse. The light was poor but she could see nobody near the building and the chain was in place. Puzzled, but reluctant to go closer, she ran back across the road to her own home and closed the door quickly behind her. It was then that she realized she was trembling.

Reasoning that if the intruder intended robbing the warehouse, he would reappear, Julia pulled a chair over to the window, sat down behind the lace curtain and waited. An hour passed and no one appeared. She was still tired and a couple of times awoke with a start to find she had dozed off. She did not know how long she had been asleep and feared that the person had left the premises while she slept. Finally morning came. By the time the sun was up she was washed, dressed and hurrying across the street. Once more the small revolver was in the pocket of her skirt.

Footprints showed in the loose dust of the alley and they led to the warehouse doors. A few early risers had already walked past the doors and obscured some of the tracks but as far as Julia could ascertain, none of the stranger's tracks led away from the warehouse. Was the night visitor still inside?

There was little point in hanging about as she was unlikely to survive a confrontation with a desperate outlaw. Returning home, Julia allowed herself a quick breakfast as she mapped out her strategy and then set out on foot for the boarding-house where she knew Black Baxter lived. Before she reached it, she saw Baxter striding toward her on his way to work. Cleary had warned her to tell no one about the night visitor, but with the lawmen absent and a possible intruder in the warehouse, she needed assistance. Baxter had always been ready to help and Julia had no hesitation about calling on him.

'Aaron,' she said when they met. 'I need your help.'

The man gave a rueful smile. 'And here was me thinking you were coming to propose to me. What's the trouble?'

Julia told him what she had seen. She was speaking nervously and a couple of times Baxter had to ask her to slow the rush of words. He listened and finally said, 'Wait here if you don't want to go near the office. I'm going back to get my gun. I won't be long.'

'I'm not frightened of going to the office.

I'll wait for you there. Carl Gustavson used to keep a shotgun there and I know how to use it. Don't be too long.'

Julia hurried to the office, opened it with the key she carried, entered and locked the door behind her. The shotgun was on a rack in a small back room with a box of cartridges on a nearby shelf. When she had loaded the gun, she felt a bit safer and went to a back window to watch the warehouse door. Black Baxter arrived a few minutes later. He had been running and was panting slightly. When he halted at the warehouse door he inspected the chain while waiting for the girl to join him.

The chain went through a hole in each of the double doors and could be turned to any position.

'The lock's not damaged and is still fastened,' he told Julia when she arrived. 'Maybe your man tried the chain and moved on.'

'If he did, he flew because there are no tracks leading away.'

Baxter laughed. 'So you've turned into an Indian tracker now.'

The girl was in no mood for jokes. 'I don't have to be an Indian to see boot tracks in loose dust. Now let's get that door open.

But be careful.'

Baxter unlocked the chain and slightly opened one door. 'Keep behind the door here as much as possible and cover me with that cannon. But be careful with it, we don't want any nasty accidents.'

'If I fire this gun, it won't be an accident. Now keep your eyes open.'

Drawing his gun, the man slipped through the door, his eyes searching for the intruder. Carefully, even appearing a little nervous, he approached likely hiding places behind the few crates and barrels that were arranged around the sides of the large shed. One by one he checked likely hiding spots and found nothing. Finally there was only a supply of baled hay stacked nearly to the roof against the back wall. He holstered his gun.

'I'll need both hands to climb to the top of this hay,' he called to Julia. 'Keep me covered.'

He was taking a risk because a gunman concealed on top of the stack could easily be waiting, ready to shoot as soon as his head appeared. Anxiously the girl watched as Baxter climbed to the top of the stack. She was so keyed-up that she only relaxed slightly when he looked around and shook his head. 'Nothing here.'

Though Julia's shoulders seemed to sag with relief she was still puzzled. 'I don't understand this, Aaron. I'm sure I saw a man go down the alley and I heard the chain rattle.'

'Did you recognize the man?'

'Last night I couldn't, but I saw him a couple of nights ago in the moonlight and he looked like your brother Josh.'

For a moment Baxter was stunned. 'It couldn't have been Josh. He has to be dead. I saw his blood at the robbery site and the bullet holes in the wagon. I wish he wasn't but I'm sure he's dead.'

Julia looked directly at the young man's frowning face. 'Do you believe in ghosts, Aaron?'

The lawmen arrived back in town around midday, tired and only partially happy with their results. They unsaddled and fed their horses before strolling across the street to a nearby restaurant for a meal. The town was still buzzing with the news of Gustavson's murder and occasionally townspeople questioned Braga about it when they saw him on the street.

The sheriff told his questioners anything that was not likely to tip off the people he

97

was hunting. He had found over his years in Santa Rosa that folks co-operated better with the law when undue secrecy was not involved. It was during one of these impromptu boardwalk interviews that Cleary excused himself and continued alone to the telegraph office. He had to give a progress report to his superiors and also seek any information available on the mysterious Sydney Bennett.

While returning after sending his messages, he noticed that the freight company office was open and called in to see Julia to find out if she could add anything to what they already knew. With the untimely death of Gustavson he knew that she would probably be busy getting business details in order so thought it best if he did not stay long. But if, by some lucky chance, he had a legitimate excuse to linger, he would be happy to do so. The more he got to know her the more he was enjoying her company.

She looked up from her work as Cleary entered and he hoped that it was not his imagination that her face seemed to brighten. 'Hello, Marshal,' the girl said. 'I hear that you and Sheriff Braga caught one of Carl's murderers yesterday.'

'That's right, but the rest gave us the slip.

I suppose you have been pretty busy here too.'

'John Barton, our lawyer, is handling all the complicated stuff but there are still a lot of loose ends. We heard that poor Mr Gustavson was shot in cold blood. Is that right?'

'It is but nobody knows why. It's possible that the bandit had a grudge against him. According to witnesses, Gustavson looked as though he was about to say something. He might have recognized the man who shot him.'

'I'm glad you came along, Marshal. I saw Josh Baxter's ghost last night again – at least that's what Aaron reckons I saw, but this ghost left footprints. I didn't think they were supposed to do that.'

'I'm not exactly up on what ghosts are supposed to do, Miss Cross, but I think you should tell me what happened.'

'I will, but first let's dispense with the formality. My name's Julia and you are Timothy, or maybe just Tim.'

'Tim will do fine. Now let's hear about Red Baxter's ghost.'

The girl recounted her experience. Cleary thought for a while and finally asked, 'Are you sure you didn't see Black Baxter? In the night you would not be able to see the colour of the hair. They both look alike according to the photo on the wall there.'

'Apart from the hair colouring, Josh had a scar through his right eyebrow, but I was too far away and it was too dark to make out small details like that. Just something about the way he moved reminded me of Josh.'

'Did Josh have a key to the warehouse?'

'No. Aaron has a key and we keep a spare key in the safe. Mr Gustavson had the chain cut in another place and put his own lock on it. He carried his personal key with him.'

'Is Black Baxter in the warehouse at present? I wouldn't mind having a look inside.'

'Aaron's down at the mule corral helping feed them at present but I can get the key from the safe. What are you looking for in the shed?'

'I don't know, but might find something if I have a look.'

They left the office and walked to the locked warehouse. Cleary could only see one lock but on Julia's instructions, turned the chain around until a second, slightly smaller lock became visible. 'So only Gustavson had a key to this lock?'

The girl nodded. Then she turned the chain around again and unlocked the regular lock. This time she was not so apprehensive as they entered the big shed and Cleary looked about. One side of the warehouse had freight waiting to be shipped out and other items awaiting collection were stacked against the opposite wall. At first glance there was nowhere that a man could really hide, but then the marshal's eye fell on the stack of hay bales piled almost to the roof. 'Do you feed your mules from this hay?'

'Not yet. It's a reserve stock that is being held for winter.'

Cleary walked to the stack, then climbed up on the bales. Standing on the top, he saw a space big enough to conceal a man against the back wall. His curiosity aroused, he looked into the space. It was only the height of one bale in depth and a couple of sacks had been spread in the hollow. It was a place where a man could hide, but apart from the sacks there was no evidence that it had been used as such. Even the sacks were ordinary grain sacks that could be found around most places where fodder was stored. He made no comment but climbed back down again.

On a shelf near the door were a few items used in the business. One was a can of harness grease. Cleary dripped a little out on his finger and went to the door. Carefully, he filled the keyhole on Gustavson's lock with the grease. 'If someone's using this lock, I want to know about it,' he explained. Then he added, 'Tell no one about this, not even Black Baxter.'

Leaving the freight company, the marshal walked back to Braga's office where he found the sheriff cursing under his breath as he consulted a pile of witness statements while trying to write his own report. 'Sorry to interrupt your fun, Lou, but I'd like to see that list we made of Gustavson's possessions. I'm curious about any keys he was carrying. I can't recall seeing any.'

'Neither can I. What have keys got to do with things?'

'Maybe nothing but some funny things seem to be happening at Gustavson's warehouse. Put your pen down for a while and I'll tell you about them.'

ELEVEN

Aaron Baxter was far from happy as he sipped his drink at the saloon that night. Until his brother's disappearance, they had drunk together each night. The pair had been bright company but now the surviving brother had grown morose and argument- ative. Consequently, a few former friends were beginning to avoid him. That night, despite having people around him, he was very much on his own. But drinking alone gave him time to think and the events of the day had troubled him greatly. He did not like people going to the warehouse when he was not there. He had been returning from feeding the mules and saw Julia and Cleary locking the doors again after they had left the shed. His first impulse had been to ask what was occurring but then he thought it might be more informative to watch and see what was happening. Accordingly he step- ped back around a corner until he was sure that the pair had gone.

Later in the day when his work brought

him to the office, Julia did not mention the incident, so he too, kept silent. For the rest of the day, he tried to guess the purpose of the visit. None of the crimes Cleary was investigating had occurred at the warehouse and the marshal's interest in the building worried him.

Though normally only a moderate drinker, he had consumed more than was usual for him and was in a truculent mood when Phil Edison walked up to the bar and ordered a drink. There was no love lost between the gambler and the two brothers. Black Baxter glared at the little gambler whom he blamed for many of his troubles. He made no attempt to disguise his dislike and frowned as though regarding something offensive. Edison had a reputation for being good with a gun but neither of the Baxters had ever shown him much respect.

A short-tempered man at the best of times, the gambler was in no mood to show politeness to any of the Baxter family. 'What are you looking at?' he demanded.

'I'm not sure,' the other said as he pretended to look closer. 'It could be a skunk but it smells worse. Could be just a low-down coyote in disguise.'

Calmly Edison placed his drink on the bar

and faced his larger and younger tormentor. Had it not been for his alcoholic bravery, Baxter might have thought twice. Instead, he gave a foolish grin when the gambler growled, 'Now, my big-mouthed friend, you can apologize or go for your gun.'

'I'm not carrying a gun,' Black Baxter said, with a smile on his face that was meant to be cunning but only succeeded in making him look foolish. 'I'm going to take you apart with my bare hands and your gun is not going to help you. If you use it against an unarmed man you'll hang for it. If you try to use that gun in any way, Braga will be down on you like a ton of bricks.'

But Edison did use his gun. With lightning speed, he threw his drink in Baxter's face, drew left-handed and laid the barrel of his .44 Russian revolver against the side of the younger man's head. His victim fell to his hands and knees and blood started welling from a cut in his jaw.

Like a cat, Edison sprang closer to his victim and raised the weapon to club him as he attempted to rise.

'Put down that gun!' Braga's voice came from the saloon doorway. He had a drawn six-shooter in his hand and an angry look on his face.

With a self-satisfied smile, the gambler put his weapon on the bar. 'Don't worry, Braga, I had no intention of wasting a bullet on him. I just decided against breaking my hands on his thick skull. In my profession a gambler who can't shuffle cards, can't work. I think I got my point across though.'

'What happened?' Braga asked the man behind the bar.

Without hesitation the barman replied, 'Black had a few too many and threatened to take Phil apart. It would hardly have been a fair fight considering the difference in their sizes. Phil did what any sensible man would do. He could have killed him, but laid him out instead. Black asked for it and sure as hell, he got it.'

Baxter was back on his feet, swearing and spattering blood on the floor as he prepared to renew his conflict with Edison.

'Take it easy,' Braga ordered. He grabbed Baxter by both shoulders. 'I thought you had more sense than that. Get down to Doc Hadlow's pronto. That cut might need stitching. And if I see you back in here tonight, or carrying a gun, you're headed for the hoosegow. Do you understand me?'

With a baleful glare the injured man

muttered, 'I understand. You're siding with him. And next time you're looking for a deputy, Lou, don't bother asking me.' Then he walked to the door and turned again. 'You're dead, Edison. We'll meet again.' An angry push at the batwings and he had disappeared into the night.

'You can put your gun away, Edison, but for the sake of peace and quiet, I'd prefer that you left town, or at least kept out of sight for the rest of the night. Black's likely to do something stupid in his present state, but he'll have cooled down by morning.'

'I don't care if he cools down or not,' Edison declared. 'I'm not scared of him or his welshing brother.'

Braga looked shrewdly at the gambler. 'Sounds like you think Red Baxter is still alive.'

'I suspect he is and will need to see his body before I'm convinced otherwise. I think his disappearance was staged. The money from those rifles and Gustavson's mules would give him a good start somewhere else.'

'But how would he carry the rifles without the wagon? Those Spencer carbines weigh more than six pounds each and there was ammunition with them too.'

'I don't know. Maybe he packed them on the mules. He could have stashed the guns in the desert somewhere till he found a buyer. You figure it out, nobody's paying me to do such stuff.'

'Be careful tonight, Edison. Black Baxter has always been a pretty solid citizen in the past but he's liquored up tonight and might do something crazy. Keep an eye out for trouble.'

After the sheriff had left the saloon, Edison nursed his drink for an hour before deciding that he would have no gamblers trying their luck against him. Aware that he could have made a dangerous enemy, he decided against another drink. If there was trouble he wanted to be sober enough to handle it. Still very much alert, he left the saloon and sought his lodgings. Halfway to the hotel he became aware that someone was following him.

The sounds were slight and indistinct. A person less vigilant would not have noticed, but Edison had lived on his wits in harsh surroundings for most of his life and had a well-developed instinct for survival.

He stopped, pressed himself against the wall of a building and looked back. In the shadows about forty yards behind him he thought he had detected some movement. If he was being trailed, the person following him remained silent and, for the present, still. The gambler paused a while but soon became aware that the man behind him had no intention of revealing his presence. After a long, hard look behind to inform his stalker that he had been discovered, he quickly moved on. A few paces later he suddenly turned again and saw nothing, but he sensed rather than saw that the unknown one was still following.

Ahead loomed the dark mouth of an alley, and it was here that Edison decided to reverse the roles of hunter and hunted. He stepped around the corner of a building, drew his gun and waited in the shadows. The feel of the saw-handled butt and the weapon's weight eased his anxiety somewhat for he was confident of his own shooting ability. With senses straining he waited watching for a sign, listening for a stealthy footfall. Now fully prepared for trouble, he was almost imagining the surprise on Aaron Baxter's face when he confronted him. This time there would be no one to interfere until he had taught his man a much deserved lesson.

But there was interference and it came

from a most unexpected quarter. Edison had made the fatal mistake of underestimating the numbers against him.

TWELVE

From the shadows across the street came a red muzzle-flash and the bark of a gun. A sledgehammer blow spun Edison sideways and he felt the numbing force of a bullet tearing into his left shoulder. Shocked though he was, the gambler heard running feet on the boardwalk and knew that the man who had been following him was closing in for the kill. Ignoring the pain that was starting to flood over him, he switched the gun to his right hand, cocked it and stepped around the corner. The move took the running man by surprise. He fired wildly but missed. Edison did not.

The gambler's bullet smashed his opponent to the ground. To be sure of his man, Edison fired a second shot into the feebly stirring body before turning to face his other attacker. But his movements now were slow and clumsy. Even as he raised his gun to fire, another shot from the hidden gunman hit him in the stomach doubling him over and collapsing him against the wall of the building.

The shooter then broke cover, sprinting across the street to fire two more shots into the gambler. He turned toward his fallen associate and knelt briefly beside him. Seeing that the man was dead, he cursed softly under his breath and fled into the darkness.

Doors were slamming and startled voices could be heard. The lamps outside the saloon revealed people spilling out into the street. The gunman, by this time had mounted the horse he had concealed behind the buildings. He was safely away before much of a crowd had even gathered.

Braga and Cleary had been working late at the sheriff's office and were among the first on the scene. They found Black Baxter sprawled on the boardwalk and Phil Edison huddled against the wall of a building. Neither had any sign of life.

'Damn fool,' Braga muttered under his breath. 'Looks like Baxter decided to even the score despite the warning I gave him. He must have gone home and got his gun after being patched up. Should have known better than to go up against a gunman as good as Edison.'

An onlooker commented, 'Black wasn't scared of much when he was liquored up. It looks like he hit Edison more times than Edison hit him.'

'They sure wiped each other out,' another observed.

By this time the gathering crowd had noted the extent of the bullet wounds. It was generally agreed that Black Baxter was a better shot than many had thought. He had scored four hits to Edison's two.

For safety's sake, Cleary picked up the fallen weapons while Braga was seeking witnesses. None had seen the shooting although many had heard the shots. They concluded too that there was no mystery about the shooting, just a personal grudge that had got out of hand.

It was an hour later, in the sheriff's office, that Cleary discovered that the incident was more involved than at first it had seemed. He was unloading Baxter's gun and found that only one shot had been fired. Edison's corpse had four bullet wounds.

Looking at the five unfired cartridges in his hand, he told Braga, 'Looks like there were two shooters who killed Edison. Black Baxter had only fired one shot.'

Later when they examined the gambler's body they found a bullet wound in the left side. The dead man had been shot from

113

both the front and the side indicating the presence of more than one shooter. Though normally a temperate man, Braga slammed his fist on the desk and swore. Could anything else go wrong?

It could, and the answer came next morning. Julia sent word that three of Gustavson's mules were missing from the company pasture where they were kept.

'It doesn't take the vultures long to start picking Gustavson's bones,' the sheriff said in disgust.

Cleary had joined him half an hour before. He looked with sympathy on the ever-growing pile of reports on Braga's desk. 'Would you like me to find out what happened to the mules while you are working on last night's mess?'

'Go ahead. I have more to worry about than mule thieves right now.'

The marshal wasted no time in reaching the freight office. He had a feeling that the theft might have been connected with Edison's killing but did not know how.

He hoped it was not just wishful thinking, but Julia seemed pleased to see him. 'Lou's tied up for a while. I suppose you heard that Black Baxter was killed last night.'

'I did. Poor Aaron. He was always so

114

cheerful and helpful. I liked him a lot. It's hard to imagine that he's gone. Is it true that he was killed in a gunfight with Phil Edison last night?'

'It's true. At first it looked as though they had shot each other, but just between us, someone else seems to have been involved. Braga's making enquiries now. He's sorry he couldn't break the news to you personally but he's mighty busy. I said I'd tell you about Baxter and help out with the company's missing mules, but before I do I'd like to check that lock on the warehouse door.'

Julia took a broad-brimmed hat from a hat stand and put in on. 'We can do that on the way to see John Somersby who looks after the mules.'

'I could handle this if you're not feeling well,' the lawman offered.

'I'll only start moping if I sit around the office. I'll go with you and we can check the freight shed as we go.'

When they examined the chain on the warehouse door, Cleary found the body of Gustavson's lock smeared with the harness grease he had put on it, but the keyhole was clear. Someone's opened this lock since we were last here.' He pointed to footprints in the dust. 'Looks like he came and went but

I'm curious to see if anything's missing.'

'Be careful. He might still be in there.'

'I doubt it, but keep out here until I call you in.'

When Julia unlocked the chain, Cleary drew his gun, slipped through the door and pulled it closed behind him. For a moment he looked around but saw that the only place where a man could hide was still on top of the hay bales. Advancing cautiously, he pulled down part of the stack rather than peer over the top. He could see at a glance that nobody was concealed in the hollow he had discovered. Satisfied that there was no danger, he called Julia into the shed.

'Nobody's here. Do you know if anything is missing?'

The girl looked around. She had a good idea of the freight they were holding. 'Everything seems to be there but something looks different.' She gazed at one wall and suddenly remembered. 'It's nothing but–'

'Something's missing?'

'It's nothing valuable or important but there were three old military saddles hanging on the wall there. Mr Gustavson bought them as army surplus for the jerkline drivers. But they were early models with rawhide covering and they soon split from

116

the weather. He bought new Morgan saddles for the drivers and I guess someone never got around to throwing the others out.' She frowned. 'Now I come to think of it, I can't recall seeing them for a while. I remember being in here the other day with Aaron and thinking that the wall looked a bit bare without realizing what the difference was. It's possible that Aaron had a clean-up and threw them out. They weren't much use the way they were.'

They left the warehouse and walked down to where the company mules were kept. There was a pasture with a few shade trees, a couple of corrals, a feed shed, a shaded feeding area and water troughs.

Somersby was waiting for them sitting smoking a pipe in one of the shady areas. He was a wiry old man as weather-beaten as the hills behind the town. His beard was grey and he had a scar on one cheek, a legacy from a bad-tempered mule. He rose awkwardly and limped toward the visitors.

'Howdy, folks. I'm glad you got my message, Miss Julia. Is it right that Black Baxter and Phil Edison rubbed each other out in a gunfight last night?'

'It looks that way, John. Gustavson Freight Lines has lost quite a few people lately. You and I and a couple of drivers are the only survivors. This is Marshal Cleary, he's here about the mules. How did you know they were missing?'

'I always count them as they come in for feeding in the morning. Some of our mules are still on the road with freight but there should be thirteen here. There's only ten. I checked the fences everywhere so they didn't get out on their own. My eyes ain't the best, but it looked like the tracks around the gate were fresh. I'm sure someone took them.'

Cleary asked, 'Was there anything special about the missing mules?'

The old man shook his head. 'Not really. They're just mules. Gustavson got 'em cheap when George Currie closed down his pack outfit. Some of the ones the thief left were much better.'

'So these were all trained pack mules?'

'That's right. You could use them in harness or under packs. There's some mules, just like some horses that won't carry packs. I seen mules you could drive or even ride that went clear off their heads if they was packed. And you need good pack harness to keep the saddle on them when they go crazy.'

'Could you tell me what these mules

looked like, John?'

'Nothin' special, two browns and a black – about fourteen hands, or maybe a bit more in the case of one of the browns. They had a GC brand on the near-side rump.'

Cleary sensed that the theft was more significant than the simple case of stock stealing that it appeared to be. He turned to Julia. 'I have to go. I have a mule thief to catch. Sorry to run out. Tell Braga what happened. I have a feeling that this could be important.'

The girl looked a little disappointed but managed to joke, 'Why is it that most of our meetings end with you running out, Tim?'

'I'll explain later. Time's important. Our mule thief could be the key to this whole puzzle.'

THIRTEEN

Cleary rode hard because he knew that the thief he was trailing would be slowed by the stolen mules. A man unused to loose-herding stock could easily have difficulty if the mules were reluctant to leave familiar territory. If he drove them loose it would take a bit of time and a lot of hard riding to get them heading in the right direction at a sensible pace. If he led them he could travel no faster than a trot until the mules learned what he wanted, and one bad leader would slow him considerably.

The distinctively shaped hoofs of the mules made tracking easy. The thief had led the animals on foot until he was well clear of the town. Then he had mounted and attempted to lead the animals beside his horse. The tracks showed that such a method was unsuccessful. At least one of the mules was not in a co-operative mood.

'He's losing time, Stonewall,' Cleary told his horse.

Next the thief had hitched the mules

single-file leading the first while the head rope of the second was fastened into its tail and the rope of the third into that of the second. Back in the old familiar routine the mules were content to stroll along, but they had learned to go steadily with packs and would not be hurried.

Cleary's grey was making light work of the pursuit, trotting and cantering, depending upon the ground underfoot, and rapidly closing the gap between them and the thief. Sweaty lather was forming on his neck and flanks but the horse was enjoying his work tossing his head and occasionally giving an enthusiastic snort.

'Just go steady,' the rider said quietly. 'We might have to cover a lot of miles today.'

The trail led out through low rocky hills sometimes crowned with rocky spires like the remains of ancient castles. Centuries of flood waters had cut deep channels into the lower ground forcing constant changes of direction but the thief seemed to know exactly where he was going. The marshal decided that it would be quicker to stay on the thief's trail rather than take short cuts and be stopped by one of the many natural barriers. Because of the broken nature of the country he could not see a long way ahead and was a little surprised when, about noon, he rounded a bend in a canyon and sighted the thief barely a quarter of a mile ahead.

A slight slackening of the rein and a light touch of the spur sent Stonewall into a powerful gallop. It was important that Cleary should be as close as possible to his quarry before he was discovered. He would never know whether the thief was careless or the sounds of the animals had masked the noise of the lawman's horse, but it was the foremost led mule that eventually betrayed his approach. The mule heard the sound, halted and looked back. The rider cursed as he felt the animal stop and looked back to see the cause of the problem. The grey horse and his rider were within a hundred yards and closing fast on him. After a moment's indecision, the man dropped the lead rope, drew his gun and turned his mount into the brush that grew thickly on the lower slopes below the rocky walls.

Cleary knew that his quarry intended to fight for there was a more open track in the middle of the canyon. He galloped past the abandoned mules and gained ground on the man who had chosen the more difficult path.

The other rider had miscalculated because

the brush where he hoped to ambush his pursuer was not as tall as he had hoped. In most places it was not tall enough to conceal a man on horseback. Briefly he considered dismounting, but the clatter of the horse's shoes on the rocks would quickly betray his position. It was too late for flight so, trusting to luck, he wheeled his mount around and charged at the man on the grey. But the ground was rough and his horse could not travel at a pace where he could use the advantage of surprise.

Cleary saw him coming and knowing that he would not be obeyed, called out, 'I'm a law officer – drop your gun.' At the same time he angled toward the other's right side. The man ignored the warning and urged his mount to greater speed. The lawman saw the muzzle of a gun swing toward him. Then with only yards separating them, he swung Stonewall to the left. The grey responded with the agility of the cow horse he once had been, allowing the marshal free movement on his own right but forcing the thief to twist slightly in his saddle and alter his horse's direction to avoid presenting a side-on target with a more limited range of movement. As he did so the approaching rider fired. The shot missed and his horse, surprised by the gun's blast, shied sideways away from it.

Shooting from fast-moving horses was never very accurate but Cleary had the easier task. Even then he almost missed and the shot aimed for the centre of his opponent's body struck him instead in the neck. The big, slow-moving bullet tore its way through an artery and shattered the man's spine making the wound doubly fatal and spilling him from his saddle.

Cleary spun his mount on its hind legs and brought his Colt up for a second shot but then saw that it was not necessary. The fallen man's hat was gone and by the red hair that was revealed, the marshal found himself looking into the dead, staring eyes of Josh Baxter. Though he had never known the man, he resembled his brother and the scar that bisected his eyebrow was proof of his identity.

'Damn fool,' he told the dead man. 'Why didn't you surrender?'

Dismounting, Cleary tried to gather what information he could by a search of the dead man's clothing. Nothing in Baxter's pockets gave any clues as to his associates, but the absence of saddle-bags or supplies indicated that he had expected to reach his home base that day. The hideout had to be somewhere reasonably close, but burdened as he was with a corpse, another horse and three mules, Cleary decided to turn back. He knew that he could not reach Santa Rosa before nightfall, so instead, made for Compton's ranch.

There was great consternation when the marshal rode in with Josh Baxter's body. The rancher had not heard of Black Baxter's death or that of the gambler, Edison, until he was told. He thought a while before saying to Cleary, 'Looks like the Baxter boys were in cahoots. Probably because Edison was after him. Red staged his own disappearance and joined up with the road agents.'

'Looks that way. With Black Baxter in town and sometimes helping out as a deputy, they had a man who always knew what Braga was doing. When we were looking for a missing bank-robber in town, Baxter hid him safely in the warehouse. No one looked there because it was all locked from the outside. Red Baxter killed Gustavson because his former boss recognized him. His eyes and eyebrows showed above his mask and that distinctive scar was a giveaway.'

'This must surely have broken the gang's back now.'

Cleary thought otherwise. 'Not really. We still don't know who is leading the gang and I still have to find those rifles.'

'They'll be in Mexico by now,' the rancher said dismissively.

'I thought that at first until Red Baxter stole those specially selected mules. He needed pack animals because, unless I miss my guess, the wagon mules he stole could not all be packed. With proper pack saddles with double cinches and breeching an ornery mule would find it hard to throw off the pack. But the thieves were using at least three old army McClellans that Red probably took in his wagon the day he set out to get robbed. These can be used for packing as long as the mule co-operates, but they are not good enough for a mule that's determined to shed its load. I'm sure that those rifles are still cached around here somewhere waiting on the right mules to carry them.'

'You could be right,' Compton admitted. 'But there's a lot of wild country around here. Where do you start looking?'

'Is Diaz still around? He has been feeding his goats all through this area. I think he could steer me in the right direction.'

'He's crazy. It's hard to make sense of anything he says,' the rancher objected. 'You're wasting your time but he had his goats down on Gopher Creek yesterday: he won't be far from there.'

'Try to keep him there. I'll be back with Braga by tomorrow night. Now, if it's OK with you, I'll turn in. I'll need to get an early start in the morning.'

'I'll tell the cook to make you an early breakfast. He has to be up early to get the stove hot. It's light about five thirty. I don't sleep too well myself so I'll probably see you in the kitchen.'

Braga looked out the office window and stared in amazement when he saw Cleary ride up to the office leading a horse with a corpse slung across the saddle.

'What in the hell have you been up to?' he asked, as he walked out on to the board-walk.

'Just bringing in Red Baxter. This time he really is dead. I had to shoot him yesterday. Him and his brother killed Edison and then Red stole those mules of Gustavson's. He probably came to town for that, but decided to help his brother even the score with Edison while he was there. I left the mules back where they belong before coming here.

127

What do you want me to do with Baxter?'

'Take him around the back and I'll lock him in a shed until the undertaker picks him up. Put the horse in the corral with ours. I'll give you a hand to unload our friend here and you can tell me what happened. There was a time when I reckoned I was the busiest man in town, but of late, Jack Simpson, our undertaker has been working harder than me.'

'You might find yourself mighty busy when I tell you what I've found out. How's Julia?'

'She's pretty shocked,' the sheriff said. 'We planted both Gustavson and Aaron Baxter yesterday. She knew them both and even if Black Baxter wasn't all good, she seemed to think that he wasn't all bad. That girl sees a bit of good in everyone. She won't be real impressed to find that you have settled Red Baxter's account. She got on well with that pair. Do you want me to break the news to her?'

'I think I'd better do it myself this time. Thanks all the same.'

After a wash, a shave, a change of clothes and a meal, Cleary knocked on Julia's door. He thought that the smile she gave as she opened the door seemed a little strained.

'Come in, Tim. You look worried.'

She directed him to a seat in a small living-room and asked in a resigned voice, 'What's the trouble?'

'I got back Gustavson's mules and found Red Baxter.'

Her face brightened. 'That's wonderful. How is he?'

'He's dead, Julia – wouldn't surrender. I'm afraid I had to shoot him.'

The colour seemed to drain from the girl's face. 'Not Josh too,' she said, as if in disbelief.

Cleary continued, 'His disappearance was staged. Him and Aaron were both working with the road agents. I am sure that Red killed Gustavson.'

'That's awful.' She tried hard to keep the shocked tone from her voice. 'It's hard to believe that the Baxters could be killers. I worked with them and liked them both and Mr Gustavson too. I could understand them killing Edison, but not Mr Gustavson. This can't be right. Surely there's some other explanation.'

'I'm afraid we finally have it right. Red killed his old boss because he recognized him during a hold-up. Red Baxter the criminal was much different to Josh Baxter the teamster. Whatever he used to be, he was a mighty different man at the finish.'

'Did you have to kill him? Couldn't you have just wounded him or something?'

'Gunfights don't work that way. You have to shoot for the biggest part of a man and hope it puts him out of the fight. Red Baxter had a chance to surrender but preferred not to take it. He knew that. I wanted to take him alive but he was prepared to kill me to escape capture. Only one of us was going to ride away from that shootout.'

'So Josh just becomes another notch on your gun butt?'

'I take no pride in having to shoot a man, Julia. Do you think I can just rest at night without things like this sometimes coming back to haunt me? I have never shot a man who didn't need shooting, but that doesn't mean that I can forget those incidents. I'm not some cold, impersonal killing machine but life would be a lot easier if I was. Red Baxter probably killed two men at the sheriff's office and he certainly had a hand in killing Edison. He might have been a friend of yours, but somewhere along the way, he became a ruthless killer. We know that Red Baxter also killed Gustavson because he had his key to the warehouse. I wouldn't waste too much sympathy on him.'

'I'm sorry, Tim,' she said softly. 'As you can see I'm not myself. It will take me a while to get used to the idea that the Baxter brothers were both killers. I could never imagine them like that and I liked them both.' She paused for a second as though to gather her thoughts and continued, 'There has been so much killing here lately and too many people I knew have been among the victims. I was talking to Chris Palmer at Mr Gustavson's funeral and he said he felt exactly the same way. He knew them all too.'

'Chris Palmer – would that be Doc Palmer, the dentist from over at Cedar Wells?'

'That's right. He comes over here occasionally and we have swapped a few books. We are both fond of reading and he seems to be the only man for miles around who will talk about books. He had a very good education back East.'

'I was meaning to see him again. He gave us some valuable information about who might be leading this outlaw gang. If he's in town at the same time as me, would you ask him to see me?'

'I'll do that,' Julia promised.

Cleary would have liked to stay longer but the atmosphere had changed. He felt that a wall had come down between them and wanted to repair the damage to their friendship. But the lawman could see that she was in no mood for further conversation so reluctantly took his leave. There was much to do in the next few hours. He would have to send a telegraphed report to his boss, attend to his horse and make sure that all was in readiness for the next day. He expected that it would be a long one.

FOURTEEN

By the time Cleary and Braga reached Compton's ranch, the owner had brought a very nervous Diaz to the ranch house. The old man was very frightened but his fears were allayed when told that his friend Braga was coming to see him. He was waiting anxiously on the porch when the two lawmen rode up.

Time was important so they got down to business as quickly as possible. The marshal would ask the questions and the sheriff would interpret the answers. Cleary's first question took the onlookers by surprise. 'Ask him how the Devil took his black and white goat.'

When the amused Braga relayed the question, Diaz became agitated waving his arms and shouting in Spanish. The sheriff spoke soothingly and asked a few more questions when the Mexican became calm again. Finally Braga relayed his answer to Cleary. 'He says that a whole army of riders came into his camp – hundreds of them. They roped his goat, tied its legs and hoisted it up on to a horse. Later he found it dead near where the wagon was robbed. They had cut its throat. But I don't think we should be wasting time chasing goat rustlers. What's your point, Tim?'

Cleary explained. 'That goat supplied the blood that was supposed to have been Red Baxter's. We all saw it near where the robbery took place and we all thought the same; just another dead goat. Now I'm rather keen to hear about those children's coffins he saw. They could have been rifle boxes. What Diaz saw and what he thinks he saw are two different things. If we can translate the imagination into what really happened, we might find out a hell of a lot. Ask him if he saw the wagon being robbed.'

'You might be on to something here,' Braga conceded, 'but making sense of it all won't be easy.' He fired another series of questions at the bewildered Mexican. These prompted a repeated outburst of arm-waving and shouting.

Then the sheriff told the others, 'He didn't see them stop the wagon so doesn't know what happened there. He was hiding out on a hill and saw the Devil and his men taking coffins from the wagon. He's sure they were the coffins of dead children. He reckoned that some of the mules were so frightened of the coffins that they bucked when they were loaded on to their backs. They threw some of them so the Devil's men could only move a few boxes at a time. It took them many trips to get all the coffins away from the empty wagon. He claims that there were at least a hundred coffins.'

'We know there were twelve boxes of rifles and two of ammunition. Sounds to me,' Cleary said, 'that he saw the gang having trouble with the mules. That would explain why you found tracks all around the area. Some of the mules were bolting and bucking and trying to throw the packs. Because of this the bandits couldn't move the boxes as easily as they had planned. I wonder if he knows where they took them.'

There was another exchange of rapid-fire Spanish and the sheriff said, 'He saw them next day. He thought he was getting away from them by going to a secret place he knew, but nearly ran into them out in the brush. He hid but saw the coffins being taken into the mouth of Hell. That took a bit of clarifying but he later modified it to mean a cave. He was pointing to the north-west so I reckon it's over there somewhere.'

'I know that country as good as anyone,' Compton growled. 'There ain't no caves over there. Could be some overhanging rocks but no caves.'

'Are you sure?' Cleary demanded.

'Wait a minute – he could be talking about an old mine. There's an abandoned mine over there dug into a canyon wall. It didn't get in very far. The Apaches killed the miners and folks say that it was salted and there never was any gold there anyway. A couple of no-goods fired gold dust into the tunnel walls with a shotgun and sold it to a party of tenderfeet. The Apaches got them all. The story is that the place is haunted.'

'Is there water and grass nearby?'

Compton scratched his whiskered chin for a while as he thought. 'There probably would be. There's been a fair bit of rain lately and I think there's a permanent spring near the mine. It would be a good hideout as long as they didn't try to graze too many horses there.'

'We know that the gang don't all hang around together so that could be why. This is starting to look interesting,' Cleary told the others. 'See what else our friend can tell us, Lou.'

After much animated discussion, the

sheriff shrugged his shoulders. 'We are flogging a dead horse now. He has no idea of numbers, his descriptions are totally distorted and he's not even sure of when some things happened. There is only one thing Diaz is sure of: there are hundreds of devils out there, far too many for us to handle.'

Cleary said, 'We know that can't be true. That gang has been considerably whittled down. We killed a few of them and they even killed two of their own. They killed the wounded bank-robber in case he talked, but I can only guess why their leader killed the one who got away with the money. Maybe the man wanted to get out or wanted a bigger share. But thieves often fall out over money. I think that as far as numbers go the Devil could not have many helpers left.'

Braga was eager to get on the trail. He asked Compton, 'Herb, would you care to guide us to this mine?'

The rancher was enthusiastic. 'Sure will. I'll bring along a couple of my men if you like.'

'They could come in handy,' Cleary said. 'But don't bring Hatton again. He's too fond of money and men like that can't be trusted.'

Compton laughed. 'He doesn't get much

chance to be crooked out here on the range but I know what you mean. Young Bill Lee was disappointed at being left out last time, so he can change places with Hatton today.'

A short while later the posse trotted away from the Spade Ranch. They made a bee-line for the abandoned mine ignoring trails and only changing course to avoid natural barriers. They skirted cactus thickets climbing boulder-strewn red ridges before descending again only to climb another ridge and repeat the process. The horses were sweating freely and occasionally the riders rested them in scarce patches of shade, but they did not delay for long. There was an expectant air among the group and both lawmen, for the first time, felt optimistic. Their mood improved greatly when they topped the last ridge and beheld a wide valley before them with a couple of distinctive mesas at the far end.

The rancher halted his horse and stood in his stirrups. He pointed to the smaller mesa on the left side. 'You can't see it yet,' he said, 'but that mine's over there near the base of that left-hand mesa. It's still a couple of miles away because this view is deceiving. The end of that valley looks closer than it really is.'

'I can't see any water.' Braga sounded worried. 'Our men won't be there if there's no water.'

'There'll be water,' Compton assured them. 'Diaz might not be too bright but he's smart enough not to bring his goats to a place without water.'

Descending to the valley floor they saw many signs that Diaz had been in the area. His goats had browsed the lower branches of some trees and a myriad of tiny hoof marks showed on patches of bare earth.

'What are the chances of the outlaws having a sentry posted here somewhere?' Cleary asked.

'They might have,' Compton admitted. 'But chances are he'll be looking in the other direction. That smoke you can see beyond the mesas is coming from Cedar Wells. They won't be expecting anyone from this direction. If we stick to the left side of the valley there is even less chance of us being spotted.'

They moved as silently as circumstances allowed, every man alert for the first sign of trouble. After rounding a spur that ran at right angles to the valley's western boundary, Compton, who was leading, raised his right hand and then pointed. A trickle of water sparkled through the centre of a grassy flat about fifty yards ahead of them. The stream was coming from a side canyon that had not been visible before. When the rancher dismounted, all followed suit.

'The mine's about two hundred yards up this side canyon,' he whispered. 'It's best if we leave the horses here.'

'Is there another way out of that canyon?' Cleary whispered.

'No. Anyone coming out has to pass us.'

They worked quickly to tether their horses in some nearby brush, then keeping to cover the men stole forward. They found themselves at the entrance to a grassy valley that had been fenced off by a temporary brush fence. Beyond it they saw six mules and two horses grazing.

The rancher tapped Cleary on the shoulder and pointed to what looked like a shady spot on the back wall of the canyon. Only when he looked at it closely, did the lawman see the mouth of the mine. He also detected movement but could not see clearly into the cavern. He was sure though that the person or persons there would have a clearer view of the posse as they advanced in the bright sunlight.

Bill Lee, their newest posse member,

asked in a low but excited tone of voice, 'Are we gonna rush 'em?'

'No,' Braga growled. 'If we do that someone is sure to get shot. The marshal and I will creep up quietly.'

There were a couple of clumps of mesquite growing beyond the fence. The foliage was not dense but would offer a slight measure of concealment.

The marshal whispered. 'I'll go first. Wait until I get to that second clump of mesquite so I can cover the cave entrance, then the rest of you come one at a time. Until it's your turn to go, keep your rifles aimed on the mine entrance. There could be one or two men there and we want to take them alive if we can. But if any shooting starts, put a few shots through the entrance just to keep their heads down.'

Compton slid up the rear sight on his rifle and said, 'I'll go last and cover the cave from here until all the rest of you reach the mesquite.'

Cleary found a low spot and eased himself over the fence. Then, crouching low, he ran to shelter behind the first clump of bushes. He half expected a shot or a challenge, but none came. Was the man at the mine simply holding his fire and waiting for a better shot?

The mesquite might shield him partially from view but it offered no protection from a bullet. He waited for a while, then took a deep breath and moved as stealthily as he could to the next clump of bushes.

But this time he knew that he had been discovered.

FIFTEEN

The grazing animals saw him and stood with lifted heads and pricked ears watching the marshal's progress. He could only hope that whoever was in the mine was preoccupied and had not noticed. He threw himself down and it was well that he did because a rifle blasted from the mine entrance and a bullet cut a twig from the bush that had concealed him.

Fortunately, Compton fired straight into the mine as rapidly as he could work the lever on his Winchester. Braga vaulted over the fence and sprinted to where Cleary was beginning to return fire.

'Keep their heads down,' Cleary called as he jumped to his feet and ran fifty yards to a pile of dirt a short distance from the mine entrance.

The rancher and his men were also pouring a stream of lead into the opening and the lawmen had to be careful to keep out of the converging lines of fire. Once safely ensconced behind the dirt, he signalled to the others to cease fire. When the rifles fell silent he called, 'You in the mine – I'm a US marshal. Throw out your guns – you won't be harmed if you surrender.'

No answer came from the mine entrance.

'Can you hear me?' Cleary shouted. 'Give up while you can.'

This time he heard a series of strange, guttural noises with a note of urgency about them as though a wounded man was trying to attract attention. Gambling that it was not a trap, the lawman ran to the side of the mine entrance and again repeated his order to throw out any guns. There was a thud and a six-shooter landed near the opening.

'You have a rifle in there too. Throw it out.'

Again there came a succession of strange sounds and it dawned on Cleary that he was dealing with a man who had been disabled by a wound. By this time Braga had joined him and Compton and his men were emerging from cover. 'Keep away from the mine entrance,' the marshal warned. 'He still has a rifle in there.'

The two lawmen looked at each other. 'What do you think?' Braga asked.

'I think he's badly wounded. I'm going in there. If all is clear, I'll call you. If you hear shooting and I don't call, you'll know I've struck trouble.'

Propping his Winchester against a nearby rock, Cleary drew his Colt. If there was any shooting, the revolver would be handier for close-range work. He knew that his sudden appearance might scare the gunman into firing in panic so he took a chance and hoped that the man in the mine was not waiting to ambush him. 'I'm coming in,' he shouted. 'Don't shoot and you won't be harmed.'

He went in quickly moving against a wall to avoid being framed in the bright light at the entrance. Before his eyes became accustomed to the darker surroundings he heard noises almost at his feet. Then he discerned the figure of a man stretched on the ground. His feet came into contact with a rifle that the wounded man had been unable to throw out.

The gunman raised his left arm in surrender. His right one had been broken by a bullet. Blood covered one side of his face and a jagged hole in one cheek showed where a bullet or probably a ricochet had smashed his jaw and teeth.

'Is there anyone else here?'

The wounded man made sounds that

Cleary took to be a negative reply. The marshal called to his comrades and they joined him around the man on the ground.

Braga recognized him. 'It's Artie Nelson. I have a lot of paperwork devoted to him. I wondered where he had gotten to. Now let's see how badly he's been hurt.'

'I was hoping that he might have been Sydney Bennett,' Cleary said as he knelt beside their captive.

The shooting had alerted the rider before he reached the mine. He was shocked because he had no idea that the law even suspected the hideout's location. Suddenly a plan conceived in certainty was thrown open to doubt. His gang members with the exception of Nelson, were all dead. It had seemed so simple to ride out and kill Nelson. Then there would be no one to connect him with the spate of killings and robberies. The stolen rifles had been safely hidden at the mine and he felt certain that he could arrange for the Mexican revolutionaries to bring their own mules to shift the weapons and ammunition back over the border. Red Baxter's plan to use wagon mules had seemed a good one but had failed in practice. Now it was time to quit. The law had destroyed his gang but he had accumulated thousands of dollars in loot even if the marshal had recovered the rifles. But there was one more problem.

Nelson was now the only threat to a perfect escape. If he was killed in the shooting all would be well, but the young desperado was not particularly intelligent and might reveal all he knew if captured and interrogated.

The rider did not enter the valley, he never did without first checking the scene from the canyon's rim. He had a small brass telescope in his coat pocket and rode to a vantage point from which to study the mine and its surroundings. Dismounting, he left his horse out of sight and concealed behind a scrubby cedar, he studied the scene.

A group of tiny figures emerged from the mine entrance. They were clustered around and seemed to be supporting someone in a red shirt. Nelson had been wearing such a shirt at their last meeting and he guessed rightly that the man was now a prisoner. He cursed his luck. At first he considered trying to silence the man with a long-range rifle shot but then reality forced him to abandon the idea. His Winchester carbine was not a long-range weapon and he doubted that he had the necessary shooting skill. Already it might have been too late. What if Nelson had already revealed what he knew?

For an hour he watched proceedings. He knew that the marshal would be making an inventory of the guns and other items the posse had found but was disappointed to see a horse being saddled for Nelson. If the man was fit enough to ride, he would be fit enough to talk. When the lawmen eventually rode away with their prisoner, they left two men on guard at the mine. Reluctantly, the watcher, who was the man Diaz had called the Devil, returned to his horse. In case Nelson talked, it would be best to leave the district or at least be ready to move quickly.

Two days later, patched up and lodged in the Santa Rosa gaol, the young gunman still had not talked. Doc Hadlow had extracted a couple of broken teeth and wired the damaged jaw but the prisoner really needed treatment that was not available at Santa Rosa. Escorted by two lawmen, he would be taken to Santa Fe. The wounded man was cunning enough to use the facial injuries as an excuse for not talking, but otherwise was co-operative with his captors.

Cleary had no trouble getting another deputy marshal to take charge of the re-covered rifles. The Federal authorities had been saved great embarrassment and were eager to show the public how well they were guarding the national interest. This left him free to concentrate upon his final task, that of apprehending the gang's leader. Unfortunately Cleary had no real description of the man he sought. Nelson seemed unlikely to talk and the one who knew the Devil best could hardly be classed as a reliable witness. His own glimpse of the bandit leader had been both distant and fleeting. One doubt was nagging at the marshal; even if he located the elusive Bennett it might still prove impossible to link him to the crimes. Replies from other lawmen in the surrounding areas could reveal nothing about the mystery man and some had suggested that the name was probably an alias. There were many men in the West living under false names for various reasons and those who kept clear of the law were very hard to trace.

Braga could not recall the man at all although, according to Compton, he had visited Santa Rosa while working at the Spade ranch. 'It seems our man is invisible,' the sheriff said.

Cleary was forced to agree but added, 'At least we know he exists because both Compton and Palmer know him. He's somewhere not far away and he has the key to this whole mess.'

SIXTEEN

With all the help he needed, Cleary set out to find the elusive Sydney Bennett. Questioning revealed a few people around Santa Rosa who knew him and to his surprise, he was told that one of these was Julia Cross. Because of a natural caution about revealing details of cases to the public he had not mentioned a name when he had asked the girl to give his message to Palmer. He would need to interview her again.

Though the freight business was all but wound up by Gustavson's lawyers, Julia still assisted them occasionally. The marshal found her at the freight office when he called there. But now she seemed a different person. The recent events had changed her from the smiling girl he had first met. For a time they had seemed to enjoy each other's company but now she had retreated behind a wall of polite formality.

The impending closure of the freighting business had left her with a very uncertain future. Unless she could find employment in the town, she would have to move elsewhere. Shocked, more than a little disillusioned by recent events and concerned for her future, her normally bright personality seemed to have deserted her. She was distant, as though talking to a stranger when Cleary questioned her about Bennett.

'I heard that you knew a man I'm looking for. His name was Bennett. Clem Summers at the bank said that you had sent him there to enquire about a job.'

'That's right. He came here looking for work. We had no vacancies but he was well spoken and appeared to be well educated so I told him to try the bank. I think he looked a bit too rough for Mr Summers so he had no luck there.'

'Do you know what happened to him after that?'

'He hung around for a couple of days and got a lift to Cedar Wells with Josh Baxter who was delivering some machinery to the mine there. Josh told me he found a job at the mine. He worked there for a while and a few months ago I think I saw him dressed as a cowhand and guessed he had taken work on a ranch somewhere around here. He was a fair way away and I could have been mistaken but I think it was Bennett.'

'You're probably right. That ties in with what I have heard about him,' Cleary told her. 'How well do you think he knew Red Baxter?' This was the first time that he had heard of a link between Baxter and Bennett.

Julia shook her head and looked as though she was tired of answering questions. 'I don't know. It's a full day by wagon from here to Cedar Wells so they would probably have talked quite a bit. Josh was a friendly soul.'

'Except when he killed people.' The words slipped out before the lawman had considered their effect. Julia looked even more miserable.

'I'm sorry,' he said quickly. 'I know that you saw a side of the Baxter brothers that I never saw.'

'Don't be sorry, Tim. You're right. There has just been so much killing lately and so many people I know have been involved. I'm not sure I can live here any more. Now I have told you all that I know about Bennett and would appreciate a little peace and quiet until I can come to terms with all that has happened.'

'I understand,' Cleary said as he put on his hat and walked to the door. Then he paused. 'If I can help in any way, I will.'

'Thank you.'

The polite but very formal reply was more in the nature of a dismissal and did not encourage further conversation.

Cleary's next stop was the telegraph office. More telegrams had come in from various law authorities around the area. None had any adverse comments about a man named Sydney Bennett. Either he had never been in trouble or the name was an alias.

The prisoner, Nelson, was still refusing to give any information that could not be signified by a shake or nod of the head. His tongue was lacerated and swollen but his captors suspected that he could have been more communicative if it suited him. Cleary and Braga had both tried to interrogate the young gunman at times, but they had learned nothing of value. Nelson would admit to nothing until he saw the lawyer waiting for him in Santa Fe.

Doc Hadlow almost collided with Cleary as he left the sheriff's office. He had been making his daily visit to Nelson.

'How's our guest?' the marshal asked.

Hadlow frowned. 'I'm not sure. He's running a bit of a temperature and his mouth seems as though it is not healing as it should. I'll be mighty relieved when he goes

154

to Santa Fe tomorrow. They can give him better attention there.'

'Do you think he really can't talk?'

'I'm not sure.' The doctor shrugged his shoulders. 'If he really wanted to communicate, I think he could do better than he has been.'

'Remembering what happened to the last prisoner held here, I'll be happier too when Nelson is safely away from here.'

Hadlow shuddered at the memory, but then said, 'I don't think such a thing can happen again. You and Braga have well and truly smashed this gang.'

'Their boss is still out there somewhere. If he knows Nelson is alive he might try to bust him out or kill him in the cell to stop him talking. I want that man before we can close this case.'

'He's probably miles away by now and still travelling. I think that things around here have become too hot for him.' With that observation Hadlow hurried away. As the only doctor for miles around, he was always busy.

Braga was also hard at work. Federal intervention had complicated some of the legal issues around charging Nelson and generated more paperwork. He begrudged time spent behind his desk but the sheriff had no way to escape it. Cleary had been able to call for assistance but his employers, the town council, reckoned that one lawman was all that Santa Rosa needed.

For a while the pair discussed the situation and both speculated upon the possibility of Nelson talking before he was taken to Santa Fe. The prisoner was their most vital connection to the gang leader but he had revealed no information about him and it seemed unlikely that he would do so.

'We're missing something,' Cleary said. 'I'm thinking of riding over to Cedar Springs when we get rid of Nelson in the morning.'

Braga put down his pen. 'That's a long ride. Are you sure it will be worth it?'

'That's the trouble: I'm not. But just maybe someone at the mine might be able to tell me a bit more about Bennett. If he's been having tooth trouble, he might have been back to Doc Palmer.'

'I think you could be having a long ride for nothing.'

'So do I,' Cleary announced as he rose from his chair, 'but I have to be sure.

'Just while I think of it, I'll check the shoes on my horse. They haven't been on that long, but I don't want to lose one on the

156

trail. I'll see you later.'

The lawman walked out on to the board-walk and saw a man hurrying toward him. He had not expected to see Doc Palmer in Santa Rosa but the dentist was hurrying as though on an urgent mission.

'Marshal Cleary,' he said in his deep southern drawl, 'I was hoping to see you here. I saw Syd Bennett this morning. I heard you were looking for him.'

SEVENTEEN

Cleary tried not to appear too excited. 'I was looking for him – wanted to ask him a few questions.'

Palmer leaned closer. 'So you think he might be behind all the trouble that's been going on around here?'

'I have no reason to suspect him of anything, but I do want to see him. Where was he when you saw him, Doc?'

'He was about five miles out of town on the road that leads out past the Spade ranch. He was riding off the road toward where that crazy old Mexican was herding his goats.'

Thoroughly alarmed that the Devil might want to silence Diaz, the lawman demanded urgently, 'How long ago was that?'

'I reckon about two hours.'

'I'm heading out there. Do me a favour and let Braga know where I've gone.' Without waiting for a reply, Cleary ran to where he had left his horse saddled in case he needed it urgently. Slipping the bit into the animal's mouth, he readjusted the throat lash and tightened the cinches he had left slack. Leading the animal out of the corral gate, he mounted and trotted Stonewall out of the town. As soon as he was clear of the horses hitched at various places along the street, he lifted the grey into a smart canter. Fearful for Diaz's safety, he was tempted to break into a gallop, but could not risk exhausting his mount at too early a stage. He geared the pace to the ground underfoot, sometimes galloping and other times trotting but never stopping until he figured that he had to be near the area that the dentist had indicated. Then he halted on a low ridge and scanned the surrounding area with his field glasses. Something white moving across a distant path of bare red earth caught his eye. Soon he could see that it was a goat. Then another, a spotted one, came into view from behind a bush. Once he knew where to look, the lawman soon found other goats grazing about. 'There are his goats,' he said to Stonewall. 'But where is Diaz?'

With a feeling of dread, Cleary cantered the grey across the plain toward the distant animals. He was about a hundred yards from the nearest goat and had slowed his horse to avoid spooking them when the old man's dog appeared. It came out of a hidden fold in the ground snarling with hackles raised and baring its teeth.

'Take it easy, old friend,' Cleary said quietly. 'I'm on your side. What are you guarding so carefully? Where's your boss?'

Then he heard the ominous double click of a revolver being cocked. Glancing to his left, he saw Diaz lying under a bush and peering at him from behind an ancient Dragoon Colt. The old man's hat was missing revealing blood in his grey hair and a wild look in his eyes.

Cleary exhausted his meagre supply of Spanish in a couple of words. *'Amigo,'* he said quickly. 'Sheriff Braga *compadre.'*

'Diablo.' Diaz said the word several times and each time became more agitated. The muzzle of the big revolver wobbled as its owner spoke.

'Amigo,' the lawman repeated as he kept his right hand raised palm outward in what was usually recognised as a peace sign. All the while the muzzle of Diaz's gun followed his every move. The hammer was cocked and the old man's finger was on the trigger. Given the weapon's age Cleary could only hope that its interior mechanism was not

too badly worn. Even a violent shake would be enough to set off some old guns and the Mexican's hand was far from steady.

Then recognition dawned. Probably because of his distinctive horse the goat herd finally seemed to associate the lawman with his friend Braga. He uncocked the gun and it disappeared into the folds of his serape. His bloodstained face broke into a smile of recognition.

Cleary pointed to the man's injured head. *'Diablo?'*

'Si.' The old man formed his fingers into an imaginary pistol and pointed at his head. Then he pointed to a bloody furrow where another bullet had grazed his left shoulder. From the awkward way that Diaz held his left arm, the marshal suspected that the shoulder could have been broken.

Signalling the wounded man to sit on the edge of a bank, Cleary took a canteen from his saddle and, wetting a clean handkerchief, set about cleaning his wounds. The head wound was caused by a bullet grazing the side of the man's head. It probably knocked Diaz unconscious at the time and the shooter had assumed that he was dead. Cleary could not ascertain whether the shoulder shot had come before or after the head wound. His patient rambled on mumbling in Spanish. Occasionally he would groan slightly as the marshal was a little rough on his wounds. The dog stood by suspiciously ready to defend its master but gradually relaxed as it seemed to realize that Cleary posed no threat.

The lawman was far from happy with the situation. He should have been after Bennett, but could not leave the wounded man. Somehow he had to get him to medical help and the process threatened to be slow and painful for Diaz.

Begrudging the lost opportunity, he assisted Diaz on to his horse and mounted behind him.

The goat herd called to his dog and the animal sprinted away to round up the flock. It was a strange procession that turned toward Santa Rosa; two men on one horse, a burro carrying a pack, a flock of goats and a dog walking back and forth behind making sure that the goats did not straggle.

Braga waited while the two US marshals loaded Nelson into a buggy and set out to meet other lawmen waiting at a distant railroad station to take the prisoner to Santa Fe. The wounded man was feverish and Doc

Hadlow was concerned that blood poisoning might be developing. Whether unwilling or unable to speak, Nelson had not imparted any information to his captors.

The sheriff was restless and wondered if he should join Cleary in his quest for Bennett but knew that the marshal had too much start on him. Reluctant to return to the paperwork and feeling hungry, he made his way to the dining-room of Pearson's hotel.

He was seated at a table awaiting his meal when Julia entered with Doc Palmer. For the first time he noticed that the dentist was carrying a gun but saw nothing unusual about that as many travellers went armed in places where bandits were known to lurk. They were talking quietly together and at one stage, the girl laughed. Of late she had ceased laughing and Braga was pleasantly surprised to hear her apparently finding some joy in life again.

The pair greeted the sheriff and Palmer asked if he had heard from Cleary. When the lawman replied in the negative, he ventured the opinion that the marshal might have had some difficulty with Bennett.

'I doubt it,' Braga replied. 'Tim Cleary can take care of himself pretty well. Maybe Bennett has travelled a long way since you saw him, Doc, but I reckon Cleary will find him.'

'Did you learn anything from your prisoner?'

'He can't or won't talk. At present he's on his way to Santa Fe. Doc Hadlow is getting a bit concerned about his wounded jaw, reckons he might need more medical attention than he can give him.'

'I know from experience that tooth and jaw injuries can have fatal results if blood poisoning appears. If that happens your prisoner could be dead in a couple of days. Too bad he's the only one who can identify the leader of the gang,' Palmer observed.

'There's still Diaz, if we can get any sense out of him.'

'I've seen him a time or two around Cedar Wells. I doubt that you will learn much from him.'

After a further exchange of small talk, Julia and Palmer moved to another table. Braga's meal arrived and, as he attacked it, he heard the others laughing together. He had read the signs of Cleary's visits to Julia and was aware that not all were as professional as the marshal pretended. As he ate, the sheriff said to himself, Tim Cleary, you have a rival and he's doing something that you have not been able to do. He has Julia laughing again.

EIGHTEEN

A few miles along the road, Cleary saw a buckboard approaching. It contained a rancher and his wife making a trip to town for supplies. Rather reluctantly, they accepted Diaz and the pack from his burro. Few would have relished the thought of carrying a none-too-clean, wounded madman but Cleary insisted.

'Leave him with Doc Hadlow,' the marshal instructed. 'I'll be along just as soon as I find enough grazing and water to leave these animals.'

Diaz raised only mild objections to leaving his flock because he was starting to feel the effects of his wounds. By signs Cleary indicated that he would not abandon the goats although secretly he would be prepared to do so if the need arose. The black and white dog made as if to follow the buckboard but the old man growled at him and shouted a few commands. The dog lowered its head and looked miserable but remained with its charges.

Uncertain how to instruct the dog, Cleary started rounding up the goats when the buckboard drove away. Much to his relief, the dog ran to assist him and drove the herd in the wake of his departing master. The marshal rode ahead and the dog kept the goats following him. After a couple of miles he found a grassy flat beside a small trickle of water. He turned off the trail and the goats followed. Soon they were lined up drinking from the stream.

'Stay there,' he ordered the dog and, to his surprise it seemed to understand what he meant. Then he turned Stonewall toward Santa Rosa and set off in a canter. Further searching was pointless. Night was falling and he would have no chance of catching up with Bennett.

The lamps were still burning in Braga's office so he paused there briefly before feeding and putting away his horse.

'So you finally got here,' the sheriff teased. 'I heard that you'd gone into partnership with Diaz.'

'It felt like it. Goat wrangling sure as hell ain't my idea of a good job. How is the old buzzard?'

'He's fine although he's worried about his goats. He's feeling sick enough to stay in bed but I had a good talk with him. I take it you didn't catch up with our friend Bennett.'

'Not a chance. Did Diaz know who shot him?'

'Sure does. The Devil did it. Diaz saw him and tried to get away. The Devil shot him in the shoulder and knocked him down. He does not remember the second shot but he's mighty lucky because it only grazed his head. But it seems that you had all the excitement. Nelson's handover went smoothly and by now he would be on the train to Santa Fe so things should be a little less worrying around here tomorrow. Hadlow was concerned about Nelson though. He thinks he could be getting blood poisoning.'

'Just our luck,' Cleary muttered savagely. 'Only two people can tell us about Diaz's Devil. One's too sick to talk and the other's crazy. It's looking more and more like Bennett's our man. I could ride out looking for him tomorrow, but it would be looking for the proverbial needle in a haystack.'

'There's someone else hit town today who might be able to tell us a bit more. Doc Palmer's in town. He's staying at Pearson's overnight, the same place as you, so you'll probably run into him in the dining-room. Getting information from him could be a slow business. He has the slowest drawl I have ever heard. But he's managed to cheer up Julia. He had her laughing today when they were having lunch together at the hotel.'

Cleary tried to sound casual but there was a trace of jealousy in his tone. 'What's he got to do with Julia?'

'They've been friends for a long time and swap books occasionally when he comes over this way. You wouldn't be getting jealous, would you?'

The denial came a little too quickly. 'Of course not. We hardly know each other. Anyway I have more important stuff on my mind right now.'

'Such as?'

Cleary thought quickly. 'Diaz's goats. They need someone to look after them – and the dog needs feeding too.'

Braga laughed. 'That's all been fixed. One of the Ramirez kids is going out to take care of the goats and he's even taking some feed for the dog. So you can rest easy. All your serious troubles are over but I reckon you have your priorities a bit wrong. I'd be more worried about losing Julia than a bunch of goats.'

'I don't own her so I can't lose her. She can see who she likes. Now I have to see to my horse. I'll call in on you in the morning and will try to catch Palmer before he leaves town.'

Cleary did not sleep easily that night. He was tired but his mind was racing and he found it hard to relax. He found himself lying awake wondering where Bennett was going and trying to piece together the situation as it had evolved. The final piece of the puzzle, the identity of the gang leader, was yet to fall into place. Sometimes, too, his thoughts turned to Julia. She had attracted him more than any girl he had ever met and for the first time in his life he was weighing up the prospects of settling down. But he knew that those prospects were fast diminishing as in Julia's eyes he was now a killer. That was a fact no matter how justified the killings had been.

Next morning at breakfast, he saw Doc Palmer in the dining-room and joined him after both had finished eating.

'I heard that Bennett killed Diaz yesterday,' the dentist said. 'Is that right?'

'Where did you hear that?'

'The word's all over town.'

'The word's wrong.' Cleary was puzzled. As far as he knew only Braga, the doctor and the couple who brought in the wounded man knew anything about the true situation. Though all had vowed to keep secret the presence of the wounded man, it seemed that somebody had become careless. Now that the word was out, there was little point in keeping secrets. 'Bennett didn't kill Diaz,' he said. 'Someone shot him a couple of times but didn't kill him.'

Palmer looked concerned. 'Thank goodness he's still alive. How is the old boy?'

'He'll live. He's down at Doc Hadlow's. Too bad he's crazy because I reckon he has a lot of important information locked up in his head. But I want to hear more about Bennett. Where did you see him?'

'I reckon he'd be about halfway between here and Cedar Wells. He seemed to be in a hurry. He didn't stop to talk, just waved as he passed me and rode on as though he had urgent business with Diaz. I thought that was a bit unusual as in the few dealings I had with him previously, I had always found him to be very sociable.'

'Can you describe him?'

Palmer thought for a while. 'He's rather thin, probably in his thirties somewhere, clean shaven. And maybe a bit taller than average. He had no coat but was wearing a black vest. I think his shirt was grey. He had a black hat on, I remember that. I'm not sure what colour his pants were.'

'Did he have a gun?'

'I think so. He usually did carry one. I'm sure he had one somewhere. He must have had one or he could not have shot Diaz, but I can't recall seeing it. Why would he shoot that old man anyway? It doesn't make sense.'

'He was probably frightened that Diaz would be able to identify him. But what about his horse?'

'I seem to remember it was an ordinary-looking bay animal, nothing special.'

'Did you see a brand on it?'

Palmer laughed. 'I'm from the East where people don't worry about brands. I know that you Westerners always tend to read any brand you see but where I came from originally, that was not considered import-ant. I'm afraid I can't help you much there.'

'So you can't add much to what we already know?'

'Not really, Bennett and I were not close friends and I have only seen him a couple of times. Sorry I could not help more but I have to get ready now to go back to Cedar Wells. You can bet there will be some miner back there waiting for me with an aching tooth. It happens every time I go away for a few days.'

'You have already been a big help, Doc, thank you.'

'I suppose you'll be going after Bennett again?'

Cleary rose from his chair. 'I have one more job to do first. I'll be seeing you, Doc.'

NINETEEN

As Cleary left the hotel something was nagging at his mind. It was only a small thing but it was a contradiction. Palmer's claim to being an Easterner did not fit his southern accent. He decided to see if Braga knew any reason for the discrepancy in the dentist's story.

'You look worried,' the sheriff greeted. 'What's eating you?'

'Just something about Doc Palmer.'

'So jealousy rears its ugly head,' Braga chuckled. 'You really are frightened that he will steal Julia.'

'It's nothing like that – just something Palmer said. He called himself an Easterner and that doesn't go with his southern accent.'

'He studied in New York. I saw his diploma on his wall in Cedar Wells. I know he's a genuine dentist. He's been one for more than ten years so he knows what he's doing. Folks around here ain't too fussy about where a man comes from.'

Cleary did some rapid mental calculations. 'By what you have told me, he finished his course around the time of the Civil War. It's a bit hard to imagine a Southerner studying in the North at that time.'

'It could happen though. Some Southerners left the South to avoid being conscripted into the Confederate Army. Folks were moving to all sorts of places in accordance with their political beliefs. Those were pretty mixed-up times.'

'That's probably the explanation,' Cleary said. 'I might have been judging him wrongly. He gave me a reasonable description of Bennett so I might send it around some of the nearby towns by telegraph.'

'I just remembered one thing though. I should have asked him what Bennett was carrying on his saddle. If there were no saddle-bags or blankets, it could mean that he is still hiding around here somewhere. I'll hurry down to the livery stable to catch him before he goes home.'

He was almost too late because the dentist emerged from the stable leading a tall, seal-brown horse. It was an animal that Cleary knew he had seen before, and in an instant the whole situation changed.

The dentist looked a bit suspicious as he

saw the lawman approaching but possibly it was only by accident that his coat was caught behind the butt of the gun on his right hip.

Cleary knew that he would need to be careful. 'Glad I caught you before you left, Doc,' he said. 'I forgot to ask you if Bennett was carrying anything on his horse, like camping gear, or stuff like that when you saw him.'

Palmer seemed to relax. He looked up as though trying to recall the meeting and eventually said, 'I don't think he had any extra gear on his saddle. Can't say I noticed any.'

'That means he's probably still around.' Almost as an afterthought Cleary observed, 'That's a nice horse you have there. Have you had him long?'

Palmer was preparing to mount and put the reins around the animal's neck before replying. 'He's not bad. I bought him a couple of years ago.'

That was all the information that Cleary needed. He drew his gun quickly taking the other man completely by surprise. 'Step away from that horse, Doc, and put up your hands. I'm arresting you.'

The dentist turned to face him and looked

suitably shocked. 'You're crazy. What's the charge – spitting on the sidewalk?'

'Let's start with murder, attempted murder and theft of government property. There could be other charges later. Now, unbuckle that gunbelt.'

Palmer flicked a glance over Cleary's shoulder. The latter saw it, but chose not to react. He could not risk taking his eyes off the man before him and doubted that the dentist would have allies in Santa Rosa.

There was a light footstep behind him and Julia's worried voice asked, 'Tim, what's wrong? What are you doing?'

'Be careful, Julia,' Palmer said urgently. 'He's gone mad. I think he intends to kill me.'

'No. This can't be right,' she protested. 'What are you doing, Tim.'

Palmer saw the distraction he needed. 'He's looking for an excuse to kill me, Julia. He's crazy.'

The marshal dared not take his eyes off the man before him. 'Please, Julia, go away. It's dangerous for you here. I'll explain later.'

'Don't believe him,' the dentist said urgently. 'He intends to kill me.'

'You may not have noticed, Doc,' Cleary told him, 'but you just dropped your fake

Southern accent. Now I know that I have the right man. I won't tell you again. Unbuckle that gunbelt.'

If Julia heard the marshal's words, they did not seem to register on her. Angrily she stepped around to confront the lawman. 'I'm not talking to your back, Tim Cleary. What do you–'

Without realizing it, the girl had stepped between the two. In a split second both men reacted.

With a powerful sweep of his left arm, Cleary sent her reeling away but the damage had been done.

Palmer was still holding his horse's reins in his left hand and with a jerk, swung the animal between himself and the lawman. At the same time he drew his gun. He fired a shot around the animal's rump. The bullet missed but the horse spun in a circle again forcing Cleary to jump back out of its path.

Then the dentist turned the animal loose and while it was still between himself and the marshal, he ran back down the street. He knew it would be suicide to attempt to mount it so close to the lawman. Another horse was hitched to a rail about a hundred yards away and he decided to try for that one. But first he had to delay Cleary.

Julia had staggered against a veranda post and with no intention of hitting her, he snapped a shot in her direction. Her cry of alarm at the near miss distracted Cleary. He risked a glance at the girl, fearful that she had been wounded. She was pale and clutched a post for support.

For a second he almost forgot about Palmer as he ran to Julia's side. 'Are you hit?' he called anxiously. A quick glance revealed no obvious injury, so without waiting for her reply, he switched his attention back to his adversary.

Palmer was sprinting down the street and already had opened up a gap of about fifty yards. Cleary sighted on his running figure but then saw that a shot from such an angle could easily finish up in the shop directly behind his target. A missed shot could result in innocent casualties and the .45 bullet was capable of going clean through a man and could still be dangerous. Almost groaning in frustration, the marshal was forced to change position so that he could shoot from a safer angle. Meanwhile, the man he was after was getting out of accurate revolver range and closer to the horse.

Few indeed are the horses that will stand when a man runs at them and the sorrel cow

179

pony was no exception. Already alarmed by the shooting, it stared in wide-eyed terror at the man's rapid approach. Then, when he was only yards away, it pulled back, broke its bridle and galloped away.

Palmer cursed the animal and glanced over his shoulder. He saw Cleary sighting his Colt on him for a long-range shot but more ominously, Braga had appeared on the scene and he was carrying a rifle. The nearest open door was the office of the lawyer, John Barton.

The lawyer saw no need to carry a gun in town and the speed at which the situation developed took him completely by surprise. He walked to the door when he heard the shooting and suddenly Palmer was there thrusting a gun under his nose.

'Get back inside – quick.'

'What are you doing? What do you want?'

'Shut the door and lock it,' Palmer ordered. A hard prod of the gun barrel in the lawyer's ample stomach reinforced the order. Given such an incentive the door was rapidly closed and locked. 'Now, where's the back door? Take me to it – move, damn you.'

Palmer could hear Cleary's boots on the boardwalk in front of the office as he and his prisoner left via the back exit. Behind the building was a stable and in that stable was

180

a fat, black horse. Barton, no longer travelled much but kept his buggy horse near his office during the week.

The dentist took up a position where he was partially sheltered by the stable wall and, pointing to some harness hanging on pegs nearby, he ordered his prisoner to put a bridle on the horse.

'But he's—' Barton's protest was cut short.

'Don't argue or I'll kill you.'

Just then Cleary appeared around the corner of the building but ducked back when Palmer sent a shot in his direction. 'Give up, Doc,' he shouted. 'You can't get away.'

'I have a hostage here,' the dentist called back. 'I'll kill him if you try to stop me leaving. Keep well back, and that goes for Braga too.'

'You can't get away, Doc. You may as well give up.'

'If you as much as show your face, Cleary, I'll kill this man and take my chances with you later. There's an innocent man who'll be killed if you even look around that corner. So keep out of my way.'

Gesturing with his gun, Palmer silently indicated that the captive should bring up the horse. Then, he whispered as he took the reins, 'Start talking. Convince that lawman

181

not to come around the corner because if he does, you're dead.'

Barton needed no urging. 'Stay back, Marshal. I'll try to negotiate some solution to this. There's no point in anyone being killed.'

Palmer vaulted on to the horse's bare back and turned it about, aiming to make his escape through a nearby alley to the street behind the main one. The animal's movements were awkward and sluggish. As the rider drummed his heels into its ribs, the horse's owner took a chance and fled. 'Don't shoot, Marshal,' he called frantically, as he ran for the corner where Cleary was waiting.

'Where is he?'

Panting for breath, Barton gasped, 'He took my horse. He won't get far: it has a bruised sole.'

Cleary sprinted around the corner in time to see Palmer kicking the ribs of his badly limping mount as he tried to turn it behind the adjoining building. 'Stop,' he shouted, as he aimed his Colt.

Palmer twisted his body and fired a shot back at the lawman. Any chance of scoring a hit was cancelled out by the crack of a rifle. The bullet ploughed into the dentist's side just as he was squeezing the trigger of his own gun. Two hundred grains of lead smashed the man from his mount and he hit the ground hard. By a great effort of will he retained the hold on his revolver and tried to sight it on Braga as the sheriff emerged from a narrow lane where he had concealed himself. But the time for warnings was over.

Braga stopped and fired again.

Palmer's body jerked under the impact, his head dropped and his face fell into the dust. By the time the two lawmen reached him there was no sign of life.

TWENTY

The next day the pair were still trying to tie up the loose ends of what had proved to be a very complicated case.

'I still don't understand how you suddenly got on to Palmer,' Braga said to the marshal. 'I was sure that Bennett was our man. I didn't realize that Doc's Southern accent was a fake one. Seems he reserved his normal way of speaking for special occasions, like killing and robbing.'

'He had me fooled too until I saw his horse. If you remember, I saw The Devil once from a distance. His horse had two white forefeet. It was only when I saw Doc's horse today that I recognized it again.'

'But lots of horses would have two white forefeet.'

Cleary smiled. 'That's what we all think. But a horse with two white feet only on the front is very rare. An old cavalry farrier-sergeant told me once that you could look through something like five hundred horses in a regiment and not see it. Those markings are extremely rare, but no one notices them until someone points them out. Certainly Palmer never knew that he was riding about on such a distinctive horse.'

'He was very smart the way he had us chasing that Bennett character. He seemed the most likely killer, 'specially as we have not been able to find him. Do you think he might have killed Bennett and hidden his body?'

'I don't know. It's possible that Bennett or his dead body might turn up one day but I'm sure that he had no real connection with this case. We spent a lot of time barking up the wrong tree.'

'Phil Edison might have been involved,' Braga suggested. 'His turning up and providing a disguise for that escaped bank-robber looked a bit suspicious.'

'We'll never know for sure but I think it was just coincidental. There was a lot of bad blood between him and the Baxter boys so I doubt that they could have worked together. I think Edison was in the wrong place at the wrong time and we were so desperate to find someone that we latched on to anyone who could remotely be considered as a suspect. At one stage I even mentioned Julia's name.'

Braga forgot his other work for a moment.

'I wonder how she is today. She was mighty shocked yesterday.'

'She had good reason to be. She suddenly lost people who were her close friends, nearly got shot and has no job now as well.'

'Julia doesn't deserve this run of bad luck,' the sheriff muttered angrily. 'Why are the good people always getting dragged down by the bad ones?'

'Unfortunately that's life. I might drop around and see if she needs a shoulder to cry on.'

'She needs one but I'm not sure she will find it here in Santa Rosa. After what happened to so many of her friends and the part we played in it, she might be a bit uneasy with us.'

Cleary thought that the sheriff might have been unduly pessimistic in his statement but it proved to be true.

'I was just checking to see how you are,' he told her when she opened the door. He could see that her eyes were red from crying and wanted to put his arms around her but she kept her distance.

'I'll be fine when things settle down a bit,' Julia said quietly although her serious manner raised doubts as to the validity of the statement.

'I'm sorry I had to push you so hard yesterday, but I didn't want you to get hurt. I could never forgive myself if you had collected a bullet.'

'There's no need to apologize. I was not thinking and created a situation where Doc was killed. Others could have been killed too. It wasn't your fault. I was wrong – just one more thing I have been wrong about lately.'

'Nobody's blaming you, Julia. Doc was not going to surrender. I think he knew he was finished and was trying to take as many people as possible with him. If you recall, he even threw a shot your way.'

She shook her head slightly as though in disbelief. 'He seemed such a gentle person. That's what I liked about him. Now I feel a fool. Was he just using me?'

'I don't think so. You're mighty easy to like. I'd say he had very good taste.'

Cleary was fumbling for words to say personally how he felt about her but, as if she could read his mind, Julia's face hardened and involuntarily she stepped back a little. An invisible barrier had descended. He had one more try. 'What are your plans now?'

'I don't think I can stay here. John Barton

187

has offered me a job but this town holds too many unhappy memories. I might move to Santa Fe and try to start over again. What about you?'

'I'll be moving on tomorrow. My work here is finished and I've been told that I'm needed in Socorro. I'm sorry things turned out like this for you, Julia, but I was sort of hoping that you would stay in Santa Rosa.'

'Why?'

'Because I want to know where to find you. I've never met a girl like you and I don't want to lose track of you. But maybe you wouldn't be interested in someone who has to be away so much. Do you think you could get along with someone like me?'

'I'd like to think that I could.' For the first time the tense look on her face softened. 'Give me a little time to think about it.'

'There's not much time left,' he reminded. 'I have to leave in the morning.'

'I'll let you know before you leave,' she said a little stiffly. 'You'll have to excuse me now.'

The marshal stepped back and she gently closed the door. That was it, so formal, like two strangers parting. Whatever might have been between them seemed to be gone.

Braga was sympathetic and that night he

tried to lighten the marshal's gloom with a couple of farewell drinks at the saloon. They had been a good team and he hoped that their paths would cross again.

A sleepless, miserable night followed with no word from Julia. He lingered about town as long as he could but heard nothing. In deep disappointment, the marshal knew that it was time to go. Reluctantly he mounted Stonewall, called to his pack mule and turned his mount for Socorro. Every step of his fast-walking horse brought Julia's house closer and reduced the time available for her to open the door. If she did not want to see him, he resolved not to knock on the door. At least she could have said goodbye, he told himself as they drew level with the house. Then the door opened and his heart gave a bound. Even though she wore an anxious expression, Julia had never looked so lovely.

The marshal dismounted swiftly, dropped his reins and with outstretched arms hurried to her. Though she had not spoken at that stage, he seemed to know that the news was good.

He closed his arms around her and, forgetting all his previous doubts, kissed her. 'You're staying in Santa Rosa?' he asked, still holding her tightly.

'I'm staying,' she whispered. 'Come back to Santa Rosa soon.'

The publishers hope that this book has given you enjoyable reading. Large Print Books are especially designed to be as easy to see and hold as possible. If you wish a complete list of our books please ask at your local library or write directly to:

Dales Large Print Books
Magna House, Long Preston,
Skipton, North Yorkshire.
BD23 4ND

This Large Print Book, for people
who cannot read normal print,

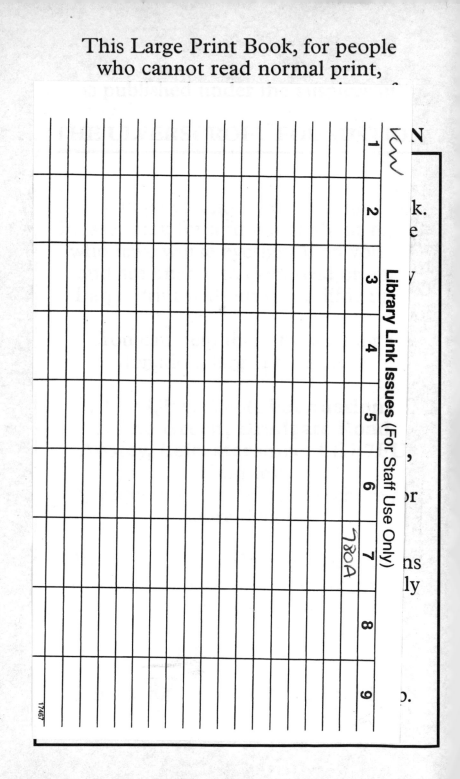

Library Link Issues (For Staff Use Only)

kw	1	2	3	4	5	6	7	8	9
							780A		

17467